Calanthe stared at him.

"But now I'm back—"

His words, so coolly uttered, stung like wasp stings on her bare arms. She felt emotion rise in her, like boiling magma. But somehow, just somehow, she kept a lid on it. She was no longer that emotional nineteen-year-old in the throes of agonizing first love. She was a mature woman. Calm, composed—under control.

My own control—

"Back for what, Nik?" she asked. Her voice was dry. As dry as sand.

Unaware that she'd called him by the name she'd used eight years ago.

He smiled. A smile that reached back through the years. A smile she had not seen directed at her for all those eight long years that divided them. That divided her stupid, foolish teenage self from the mature, capable, self-controlled woman she now was.

"For you, of course, Calanthe," he said.

Julia James lives in England and adores the peaceful verdant countryside and the wild shores of Cornwall. She also loves the Mediterranean—so rich in myth and history, with its sunbaked landscapes and olive groves, ancient ruins and azure seas. "The perfect setting for romance!" she says. "Rivaled only by the lush tropical heat of the Caribbean—palms swaying by a silver-sand beach lapped by turquoise waters... What more could lovers want?"

Books by Julia James

Harlequin Presents

Visit the Author Profile page
at Harlequin.com for more titles.

Julia James

RECLAIMED BY HIS BILLION-DOLLAR RING

HARLEQUIN

PRESENTS

ISBN-13: 978-1-335-58432-8

Reclaimed by His Billion-Dollar Ring

Harlequin Enterprises ULC
22 Adelaide St. West, 41st Floor
Toronto, Ontario M5H 4E3, Canada
www.Harlequin.com

Printed in U.S.A.

Recycling programs for this product may not exist in your area.

RECLAIMED BY HIS
BILLION-DOLLAR RING

Happy memories of our first family Greek holiday

PROLOGUE

CALANTHE STOOD BESIDE her father, greeting their guests for the evening as they arrived in the banqueting suite of this top Athens hotel. All of Athens high society was here, and she was glad of it. Her father's sixtieth birthday was something to celebrate after all.

Her glance went sideways to him, a small frown forming. For all his bonhomie there was a look of strain about him, and his shoulders sagged as if he were making a visible effort. He did not look well.

Anxiety plucked at her. Her father had always been an ebullient character, strong-minded and forceful—characteristics that had made him a very wealthy man, whose property empire was worth a fortune. Though her own specialism was classical art, and she split her time between museums in London and Athens, Calanthe knew that as her father's only child she would one day inherit all his wealth. But she did not want that

day to come too soon. She wanted her father t
live longer than her mother had.

Grief shadowed her face… It was barely tw
years since her English mother had succumbe
to the cancer she had fought so valiantly.

She shook the sadness from her. She was her
as her father's hostess and she wanted to d
him proud. She had already received approvin
smiles, and his praise of her had been heartfel

'My darling child, how beautiful you look!'

If she did, it was for him, she knew. For h
position as the daughter of Georgios Petranako:

She was gowned in a couture number, its pal
blue silk a match for the grey-blue eyes inherite
from her mother. Her dark hair and Mediterra
nean complexion came from her Greek gene:
The artful bias cut of the gown showed her sler
der figure to perfection. With her perfect ov:
face, delicate nose and tender mouth, her hai
in an elegant upswept style and her father's gi
of a simple yet extremely expensive diamon
necklace around her swan-like neck, Calanth
knew that her beauty was assured.

It drew eyes and attention—and always hac
But her smile was never more than gracious, he
air always a little elusive. It exasperated her fa
ther, she knew. He wanted her to marry—an
soon. But to marry required falling in love—

and she had done that once before, when she had been young and naïve and trusting.

And she had her heart not just broken, but smashed to pieces—her illusions shattered in the cruellest way.

More guests were arriving, and she made herself pay attention to them, exchanging social chit-chat, being her father's gracious daughter as always. Soon they were moving away, and her eyes moved once more to the entrance to the banqueting suite, where new arrivals were being ushered in by the hotel staff.

One of the waiters glided up, proffering fresh glasses of champagne, and absently, with a smile of thanks, she took one, handing one to her father as well, while he conversed affably with yet another guest. Calanthe's gaze flicked back to the entrance. Surely everyone who had been invited was here by now? Dinner—a lavish buffet in the adjoining room—would soon be served.

She was just about to take a sip of her champagne when another guest made an appearance. Tall, wearing a tuxedo like all the other male guests, his face was averted from her as he spoke to a member of staff on the door. But there was something about him…

Suddenly, out of nowhere, every muscle in Calanthe's body tensed. Her breath froze in her throat, fingers convulsing on the stem of the champagne flute.

The new guest turned…looked into the crowded room.

Faintness drummed through Calanthe and she felt the blood drain from her face, a deathly coldness seize her.

CHAPTER ONE

Eight years earlier

GINGERLY, CALANTHE EASED up the ceramic shard embedded in the hard, dry earth, delicately teasing it free with the tip of her trowel, calling across to Georgia, working beside her, to take a look with a more expert eye than her own.

It was Georgia who was studying archaeology, and was therefore well experienced on digs, whereas Calanthe was reading History of Art, which was a lot less hands-on with its subject matter. But she'd happily volunteered to join the student team which Georgia's professor had pulled together on a very tight timescale, to excavate a site newly revealed by the construction of a holiday resort on one of the myriad islands in the Aegean.

The students were a cheerful crowd, glad of a free, albeit working holiday in Greece—

a sunny change from their *alma mater*, a rainy north country university in England.

Calanthe was pitching in willingly. She might have a wealthy Greek father, whom she'd visited twice yearly all her childhood, enjoying staying with him at his luxurious mansion on the outskirts of Athens, but she'd been raised in a quite ordinary way by her mother. Few knew she had a Greek surname as well as the English surname of her mother, which she was known by, and not even her close friends knew just how rich her father was.

'What do you think?' she asked Georgia now, holding the curved terracotta shard in the palm of her hand.

Georgia peered at it. 'Possibly Corinth ware? Let's see if there's more before we tell Prof,' she said enthusiastically, and set to with her trowel and brush.

A shadow fell over their kneeling forms.

'Find any gold or jewellery yet, ladies?' a deep voice enquired laconically in accented English.

Startled, Calanthe and Georgia lifted their bowed heads. Simultaneously, Calanthe was dimly aware, both their jaws dropped. The stranger looking down at them in their shallow trench was totally worth the reaction. Calanthe felt her breath catch. He stood there, towering over them—and not just because they were

neeling in a trench—booted feet apart, long
:gs encased in multi-pocketed khaki work trou-
:rs, heavily belted. He was narrow-hipped and
road-shouldered, his obviously muscled chest
noulded by a dusty khaki tee, and he sported
ark glasses that only emphasised the strong line
f his jaw, already starting to darken this late in
1e afternoon, the sculpted mouth and the blade
f a nose, and the dark, slightly over-long hair
nat feathered over his brow and at the nape of
is strong neck.

The whole package was rough, tough and to-
ally devastating...

Calanthe heard Georgia gulp and knew why.

'Just pottery so far,' Georgia managed to get
ut, scrambling to her feet.

Calanthe found she was doing likewise, sud-
lenly burningly conscious that her comfy but
aggy shorts were covered in soil, her own
:e shirt damp with sweat, and her plaited hair
crewed up unflatteringly on the top of her head.

Who *was* this guy? she found herself think-
ng, then answered her inchoate question herself.
'retty obviously, he was one of the workmen
rom the hotel construction site nearby. A sec-
nd later she confirmed it—he was holding a
ellow hard hat in one hand. However, what he
vas doing over here at the dig she had no idea.

The excavation was out of bounds to all but the archaeology team.

'You're not supposed to be here,' she heard herself saying. It came out in a clipped voice, but that was from disconcertion, not in reproof.

Had he taken it as the latter? Something about his face seemed to harden a fraction, and even though he was wearing sunglasses Calanthe felt his gaze pierce her. She gulped, like Georgia, though hopefully more quietly.

'I was curious,' he informed her, in the same laconic fashion with which he'd asked his original question. 'This is, after all my country's history you're digging up,' he went on, and now his voice was less laconic, 'Not your own.'

Calanthe felt the pointedness of his remark and her chin lifted.

'Perhaps your country,' she said, echoing his tone deliberately, 'might show that it values its history more by banning the building of hotels all over it!'

This time the veiled gaze was definitely directed at her.

'The excavation site is being protected,' he shot back. 'And modern Greeks have to earn a living. Tourism is a major revenue source, so hotels are not a luxury but an essential necessity.'

His glance went to Georgia, and Calanthe felt

as if she'd been dismissed from his attention. She wanted to bristle—but what he'd said was true.

He was speaking again, his voice back to being laconic now. 'I was wondering if you could do with another volunteer, maybe, when I get off my shifts?' He glanced back at Calanthe, who felt herself flush again, and hated herself for it. 'Given the tight time scale you're working under.'

'You'll need to ask Prof,' Georgia said. 'He's over there.' She pointed.

The stranger nodded. 'Thanks. I will.'

He strode off, and Calanthe sank down on her knees again, deliberately not watching him stride away.

Georgia did, though—quite shamelessly.

'Oh, *wow*!' She heard Georgia sigh. 'Whatever he's got, he's got it two hundred per cent!'

'He's just a brickie,' Calanthe snapped.

Georgia's eyebrows rose. 'That sounds pretty snobbish,' she observed.

Calanthe shrugged. 'Well, what would some guy off a building site know about what we're doing?'

'He's interested,' Georgia said. 'Give him a chance.'

To do what? Calanthe heard the question in her head and didn't like that she'd asked it. Or wondered what the answer was.

'He could be wanting to filch stuff,' she ar
gued. 'After all, he asked if we'd found gold o
jewellery!'

'Everyone always asks that at digs,' Geor
gia replied mildly. 'Anyway, we're not going te
find gold and jewellery—just pots. Speaking o
which…let's see if we can find the rest of tha
pot. Come on—get stuck in!'

Calanthe did so with a will. It helped to pu
out of her head the workman who'd just volun
teered to help out. But not, to her annoyance,
very effectively.

Georgia, damn it, had been right. Whatever
the man had, he had two hundred per cent of it…

His name, so Georgia informed her that evening,
when they set off with the other students to the
cheap taverna near the harbour, was Nik.

'He's going to be working with Dave and
Ken—when he can spare the time from being
a *brickie*,' she said, pointedly using Calanthe's
snobby description to mock it.

'Rather them than us,' answered Calanthe.

'Oh, come on—you're transparent!' Georgia
quipped. 'You're only saying that because you
fancy him rotten and don't want to admit it!'

Calanthe's face set, but Georgia wasn't done
yet.

'Well, I fancy him rotten too—the voice alone,

with that to-die-for accent…let alone the rest of him! But I'm honest enough to admit it. And…' she gave an exaggerated sigh '…also honest enough to know that I don't stand a chance. He's way out of my league.'

Calanthe snorted. 'Don't do yourself down!'

'I'm not,' said Georgia. 'I'm just being honest. Besides, I came out here hoping me and Dave might get it together—I've been after him for ever! On the other hand,' she mused as they gained the harbour area, glancing at Calanthe, who was looking a lot less dusty and work-worn now, in a loose-fitting cotton shift dress that skimmed her slender figure very nicely, her hair caught back in a ponytail that gleamed like mahogany, '*you*, my girl, definitely *are* in Nik the Greek's league! Nik the *Gorgeous* Greek…' She sighed extravagantly.

Calanthe snorted again. 'I have absolutely *no* interest, thank you—'

'Well, he'd be interested in you, I'll bet, with *your* looks! Greeks always fall for cool English girls! Of course, you're half-Greek yourself—I keep forgetting.'

'Georgia, please don't mention my Greek side to your precious Nik the Greek—'

Calanthe threw her friend a seriously warning look. She didn't want any questions about just who her father was. The surname was well known—and the wealth that went with it.

'Yeah, yeah… OK, I promise,' Georgia assured her airily. 'Now, come on—let's find the others and get some food. I'm starving.'

They quickened their pace, catching up with the others as they reached the quayside taverna which they frequented every night.

Joining the group of students—their professor and his deputy dined elsewhere, knowing their presence would only be restraining—Calanthe settled into the cheerful crowd, ordering a beer with the rest of them. Soon carafes of local wine and the usual local fare of *gyros* and *souvlakis* were all demolished. Conversation was lively, irreverent and familiar—discussing the day's dig and other archaeological matters, then segueing into universal topics of interest to their generation, from bands to politics to averting catastrophic climate change.

Their long table was outdoors, in the evening's cooler air, and everyone was relaxed and convivial. Calanthe sat back, glass in hand, wondering if she had room for one more of the sweet, sticky pastries that were the traditional dessert at tavernas such as this. She made a slight moue. Her father would be astounded to think of her dining in such humble surroundings. When she was with him in Athens fine dining was the order of the day, without exception, whether that was at home, courtesy of his in-house chef, or at the city's most expensive restaurants.

A wry smile tugged at her mouth as she took another mouthful of the wine, letting its rough but rich warmth fill her, enjoying the light breeze picking up and the sound of the sea lapping at the small boats in the harbour. She dipped her neck, rolling her shoulders slightly to release the muscles that had been hunched most of the day as she'd worked beside her fellow excavators.

'Need a massage?'

The low, deep voice spoke behind her. Laconic and accented. And familiar.

She jerked her head round, her expression altering immediately.

He might not be in his work clothes any more—he'd changed them for jeans and a fresh tee—but there was no mistaking who stood there. Tall, dark and devastating…

She felt a gulp form in her throat and suppressed it. *No*, she would *not* respond to the ridiculous impact this wretched man seemed to have on her—and every other female too. She was aware that Georgia had suddenly looked up from what had seemed to be a more-than-friendly tête-à-tête with Dave across the table, not to mention several other women further along, who were suddenly craning their necks to look at the tall figure now standing at the far end of the table.

'Nik—hi. Take a seat!' Ken called out from a few chairs along, waving in welcome.

To Calanthe's annoyance—and just why she was annoyed she didn't particularly want to think about—Nik casually swung a spare chair from a nearby table, and sat himself down, happy to let Ken reach for an unused glass and pour him a glassful of wine from the carafe.

'*Yammas...*' Nik said in the same casual fashion as he helped himself to the glass.

He glanced around the table, and then his gaze settled on her—again to Calanthe's annoyance, and this time she was more aware of the reason for it.

He tilted his glass at her. 'To finding treasure,' he said.

There was a glint in his dark eyes—eyes she would have preferred to still be shaded by sunglasses. Because unshaded they were...

She gave a silent gulp.

Dark and devastating, just like the rest of him...

Then he was saying something else. Not in English this time, but a murmur in Greek. She stilled.

'But I think I've just found it. Golden treasure...'

With an effort of intense will she kept her expression blank, as though she had not understood
what he'd just said.

Or what he'd meant.

If she'd had any doubt, the glint in those dark
and devastating eyes deepened, the sudden brush
of his long lashes veiling it, but not before she'd
read the meaning in it as clearly as she'd heard
the words he'd just said.

For a second—or was it far longer than that?—
she could not move. Not a muscle. Only sit there
while those incredible eyes washed over her.

Marking her out…

For himself…

Out of nowhere, she could suddenly hear her
own pulse, her own thudding heartbeat. Hear it
and know why it was so suddenly, overpower-
ingly audible.

Then, breaking the moment, and breaking the
look he was giving her, Georgia spoke.

'No treasure, Nik,' she said with a laugh. 'Just
pots. And some bronze, if we're lucky.'

The dark, devastating gaze left Calanthe and
she felt she could breathe again. Shakily, she
reached for her wine, feeling the need for it.

What the hell had just happened?

She didn't want to think about it. Wanted to
make herself listen to what was being exchanged
now…just stuff about the excavation.

Nik had clearly picked up on what Georgia had said. 'Bronze? No iron, then?'

'Maybe some,' Dave put in. 'But Prof says this site is likely to be on the cusp, timewise, between bronze and iron. Probably eleventh... maybe tenth century BC.'

Nik nodded. 'OK, so post-Mycenaean, then? More Dark Ages, pre-Archaic?'

Calanthe glanced at him, open surprise in her face at the knowledge he'd just displayed. For her pains she found herself on the receiving end of another glinting look from him. He was clearly aware of her surprise, and why it was there.

But now Dave and some of the others were launching into a discussion of just when the site might prove to date from, and what the implications of its location might be.

Nik, it seemed to Calanthe, was holding his own, although he was clearly no specialist. He made some remarks about building styles and methods in use in the period, and then Calanthe heard herself speak.

'You seem to have picked up a bit of historical knowledge by working on a modern construction site!' She spoke lightly, as if humorously, but his response was to throw another glinting look at her.

'No,' he replied pointedly, 'what knowledge I have of historical building styles and methods

I've gained on my degree course in architecture—I did a module back in my third year on Classical Greek architecture.'

Calanthe felt her face stiffen. It had been a put-down, clear and obvious.

And I deserved it. I put him down first, implying I was surprised that he should know anything intellectual since he's only a brickie on a building site...

She picked up her glass, knocked back a mouthful of wine as a diversion, wondering why she'd felt the need to speak as she had. Seeking to keep him 'in his place'?

To keep him at a distance—that's why I did it. Because...

Her glance stole to him again. She heard him laugh at something one of the others had said, his dark head thrown back, his smile open and ready, displaying strong white teeth and carving lines around his mouth, crinkling his eyes.

Calanthe felt her breath catch. He really was the most incredible-looking guy… With a sigh of defeat, she admitted it.

Georgia had turned away, diverted by Dave, and Calanthe leant forward, leaning her elbows on the table, wine glass in her hand, sipping from it, giving in to what she wanted to do. Just sit there and gaze at him…

After all, why *not* let herself gaze at him
Admit how gorgeous he was?

It was harmless enough, wasn't it?

Quite harmless…

Athens: the present

Harmless…

The word tolled in Calanthe's brain now, a
she stood beside her father.

No, it had not been 'harmless' to indulg
as she had wanted to do—as she had actual
done—that long-ago summer, a wine glass lazil
in her hands, letting her dreamy, wine-infuse
gaze self-indulgently rest on the man seated fu
ther along the taverna table, drinking him in a
if he, too, were wine…

It had not been 'harmless' to have anythin
to do with him at all. Let alone—

She silenced her own inner, anguished voice
What use to tell herself what she should hav
done all those years ago? She hadn't—and he
stupid, trusting heart had paid the price for i
She had been broken, and bitterly disillusione
by the man he'd turned out to be.…

She heard, in her head, the echo of her father'
voice, telling her just what Nik had done…wha
he had stooped to. How shamelessly, readily h
had done so.

She tore her mind away—it was in the past and she would keep it that way.

Except that the past was now walking towards her. Purposefully heading towards her father and herself.

She had moments only to brace herself, to dredge up strength from somewhere deep inside her, and then he was there. Standing in front of her, a bare metre away. As tall and as head-turningly good-looking as he had ever been.

His evening dress was bespoke, hand-tailored to his broad, strong frame, superbly moulding his superb body. His hair was cut short and by an expert, feathering at the nape. His jaw was pristine, his skin smooth. He was svelte, groomed, immaculate, fitting in seamlessly with all the other svelte, groomed, immaculately clad rich men around him.

He stood in front of her. The eyes resting on her, not her father, were as dark, as long-lashed and as unreadable in their depths as they had ever been. With nothing in them except the bland civility befitting the occasion.

All her strength was going into standing there, every muscle taut, her fingertips tight around the stem of the champagne flute so that the skin around her lightly varnished nails was white. She had no strength left to analyse the something

that flared to life in those unreadable depths—
something that was not bland at all.

But then it was gone, and now he was speaking, that same bland civility in his voice.

'Hello, Calanthe, it's been a while.'

CHAPTER TWO

NIKOS SAW HER FREEZE. Saw shock flash fleetingly across her face. Well, he hadn't been expecting to see her either. It had been impulse only, his instinct for taking opportunities as they presented themselves, that had made him walk in here.

His eyes went past Calanthe to the man beside her, who had registered his presence and now paused in his conversation with the man he'd been talking to, who nodded and moved away. There was a questioning look in Georgios Petranakos's eye, and Nikos spoke to allay it.

Even as he did he was conscious of a sense of biting irony. Georgios Petranakos had no idea who he was. The fixers he'd despatched eight years ago to protect his daughter would have recognised him, despite the different name he'd used back then...

Well, he was using his own name now.

'Nikos Kavadis,' he said, introducing himself.

He saw Georgios Petranakos mentally review the name, then nod in recognition. 'Ah, yes,' he said.

'I hope you will not mind my intruding like this, Kyrios Petranakos.' Nikos gave a smile that was a judiciously exact blend of confident and respectful. 'But I'm staying at this hotel at the moment, and I noticed your name listed on the function board in the lobby.'

The older man smiled genially. 'I am very glad you can join us.'

Nikos's social antennae, long honed, caught the note of genuine welcome in his host's voice. And, after all, why should he *not* be welcome?

His eyes darkened momentarily. Once, he would never have been welcome. Once, steps would have been taken—*had* been taken—ruthless and swift. His mouth twisted. Highly effective steps to dispose of him promptly.

But now... Oh, now he was completely eligible to move in such elite circles as Georgios Petranakos did. OK, so his own business affairs were not centred in Greece but ranged globally, wherever his specialist, innovative services were required—services so specialist, so innovative, that they had made him, in eight short years, a very wealthy man.

A man who could walk in, uninvited, to a rich man's private party with impunity. A man who

ould, with equal impunity, let his gaze go to the
woman standing at Georgios Petranakos's side.
A woman he'd had no idea he would set eyes on
again. A woman he had once known, eight long
years ago, as a very different person.

*But she was always the woman I see here
now! Even back then.*

His thoughts darkened.

*But back then I did not know who she was.
Not until—*

He pushed these thoughts away. When
he'd found out who she was, everything had
changed...

But as his gaze rested on her now he knew,
with a surge of his blood, that one thing had not
changed. A kick went through him, visceral and
compelling. As visceral and as compelling as it
had been the very first time he'd ever set eyes on
her. Though here, in her couture gown, with her
immaculate upswept hair, her perfectly made-up
face, diamonds glinting at her throat, she could
not have looked more different from the way he
remembered her.

And yet...

*Her beauty is the same—as perfect now as
it was then...*

He felt emotions well up in him—and memories... oh, definitely memories. Sensual, evoca-

tive and, sweeping over him in a way that was so very, very pleasurable…

For a moment he indulged them, gave them space to possess him. But then other memories came too. Memories less pleasurable. Unwelcome and jarring.

Georgios Petranakos's fixers…making me that offer…spelling it out to me.

Again, he pulled his thoughts away. His host was speaking, and Nikos gave his attention back to him, glad to pull away from thoughts he did not want to have…unpalatable memories.

'My daughter Calanthe,' Georgios Petranakos announced.

Had her father heard his murmured greeting a moment ago? Nikos gambled that he had not. Gambled, too, that Calanthe would make no reference to their prior acquaintance.

Acquaintance? The word mocked him silently inside his head. What he had had with Calanthe that summer long ago had been so much more than an 'acquaintance'…

'Kyrios Kavadis.' Her voice was cool, her expression cooler.

Yet she wasn't cool at all.

Nikos knew it. Could see it in the stiffness of her slender body, the way she held her head so high, the blankness in her face, her eyes. He felt again the emotions—untidy, irrelevant, unwelcome—that had made their presence felt as he'd walked towards her. As he'd registered her presence here, and that their paths were crossing like this after so long.

His gaze washed over her, expertly assessing. Eight years ago, not even out of her teens, she had had the natural loveliness of youth, but now...

Now she has come into her full beauty.

Exquisite—that was the only word for her now. The word echoed in his head. She was as exquisite in her beauty as her couture gown was exquisite, as the delicate diamonds at her throat and earlobes were exquisite, the diamond clip in her upswept hair. Chic and soignée, poised and elegant.

Memory thrust into his vision. Her coltish body in shorts, exposing her long, tanned legs, and a clinging tee shirt that moulded her breasts. Her hair in a plait hanging down her back, ready for a day working on the dig.

Then later, heading off to the taverna in a colourful, calf-length gathered cotton skirt and embroidered blouson, showing off her sun-kissed shoulders, her hair loosened into a tumbling cloud.

And later still, when he had taken her back to his room in the cheap *pensione*. Her lovely face lifted to his, her mouth tender as a newly rip-

ened peach, her naked body arched and arder
beneath his, long limbs twining intimately wit
his, her hands winding around his bare back a
he moved to take sweet possession of her…

Memory quickened in him.

And more than memory.

Desire.

It rose within him like a rich, potent liqueu
bringing the past into the present, fusing i
melding it, dispelling any doubts that had pulle
at him moments ago as to whether it was wis
to see her again like this. See her again afte
so many years. Here in her own refined, be
jewelled milieu, a million miles from how she'
been when he'd first known her.

Yet again emotion plucked at him, unwelcom
and jarring, but yet again he set it aside, dismiss
ing what he did not wish to feel. Right now a
he wanted was to let his gaze feast on her as sh
stood there, the poised and perfect daughter of on
of Greece's richest men, taking in her exquisit
beauty, savouring it, melding it with his memorie:

But his host was addressing him once mor
Requiring his attention.

'So what brings you to Athens? You are head
quartered, I believe, in Switzerland?'

'Yes,' Nikos acknowledged, wresting his gaz
and his mental focus away from where it wante
to be. 'Zurich. But I am here in Greece at the gov

ernment's invitation, to consult on the current parliamentary enquiry—which of course you will know about—into reducing the cost of affordable housing whilst ensuring it is both environmentally low-impact in its construction and maintenance as well as earthquake-proof. It's based on work my company has undertaken recently in the Middle East, where similar constraints operate.'

He saw Georgios Petranakos nod knowledgably. 'Ah, yes, of course. I, myself, am likely to be involved marginally—though my remit is commercial rather than environmental.' He nodded. 'Perhaps we may find some discussion useful to us both while you are here?'

Nikos smiled politely with satisfaction. 'I would be more than happy to do so. When might suit you?'

'Come for lunch,' his host said expansively. He turned his head towards his daughter, who was standing rigidly, holding her glass of champagne. 'Calanthe, my darling one, you know my social diary better than my PA! Can we fit young Kavadis in for lunch this week? I was thinking, perhaps, of the day after tomorrow?'

His daughter's expression did not change. But Nikos knew with every fibre of his being that her father's invitation was not welcome to her.

That was understandable.

Again, memory pulled at him—but still he would allow it no ingress.

She did not blink. 'You are seeing your cardiologist that morning, Papa,' she said. Her voice was tight.

Georgios waved his hand impatiently. 'Plenty of time to get home for lunch!' he said airily. Then he turned his attention back to Nikos. 'We shall see you then?' He smiled genially, but dismissively.

Nikos nodded, the gesture encompassing Calanthe as well, and murmured his thanks. Then, knowing he had used up his host's attention span, he strolled away.

He was done here for tonight.

Thoughts flickered behind the unreadable mask of his face. So that was Georgios Petranakos in person. And *that*—once more that mix of honeyed memory and jarring awareness twisted in him—was his daughter Calanthe, in person.

Her name echoed in his head. He had had no thought of her when he'd followed his impulse to make himself known to her father. Yet now that he had seen her...

More beautiful than ever.

Eight years ago he had made the decision and done what he had done. But now the years had passed, changing so much, and what he had once let go of had just come into his life once more.

All his life he'd seized opportunities as they'd

come by. It had taken him from a frugal rural life on a small Aegean island to diligent studying at school and entry to a lengthy architectural degree, on to venturing into business for himself, seeing those opportunities and capitalising on them, in the process making himself a wealthy man.

The journey had been intense and demanding, absorbing all his energies.

He had seized at those pleasurable carefree weeks with Calanthe just as he had seized at all the opportunities that came his way. And then the currents of his life had taken him onward...

And now they have brought Calanthe back into my life. Into my reach.

And this time...

His dark eyes glinted. Resolve filled him. A decision took shape in his mind.

The past had gone. But the present—oh, the present might yet be claimed for himself...

And this time—*this* time—there was no impediment to indulging that claim.

Calanthe lay in bed, her sleepless eyes staring upwards. Out of nowhere, with no warning, the past had opened up and walked into the present.

Nik. The man I gave myself to—gave my stupid, stupid heart to. The heart he not only tossed aside but...

A wash of humiliation swept over her. She

had not felt it for years and yet it was here now, again, hot and humid and hideous. She could not bear to feel it…to remember it. To remember how her father, seeing her shed unstoppable tears over the man who had walked out on her, had taken her hands in his and told her just *why* Nik had walked out on her…

She heard her father's voice, kindly, but adamant.

'A man who could do that, my dearest girl, is worth no tears—no tears at all!'

She felt her face contort. No, Nik was worth no tears—yet she had shed them all the same.

She felt her hands clench at her sides in anger and in impotence. Then, deliberately, she stretched her fingers out, though they did not want to do so. Deliberately, she took a scything breath and set her mouth, a hardness forming in her unseeing eyes.

So Nik had walked back into her life again. The cold, disbelieving shock she'd felt as he'd headed towards her hammered into her once more. But she would not—*would not*—let him in again. She would keep him out with all the strength she possessed.

Her face twisted.

He will never hurt me again—never. I won't allow it. I won't permit it. I won't ever be vulner-

*ble to him again! Because I know him now as I
'd not then. I know him for what he is.*

That knowledge must keep her safe. It *must.*

Yet for all the bitterness that filled her, so did
much, much more…

With a low, anguished groan she went on staring blindly at the ceiling, misery and memory
filling her.

'Papa, what did the doctor say?'

Calanthe was waiting in the plush waiting
room of the exclusive clinic where her reluctant
father had been persuaded to see his eminent
cardiologist.

'I'm perfectly fine! Just as I told you I was!'
came the testy reply as her father marched out
of the clinic into the waiting car.

'Really?' Calanthe said, not hiding the scepti-
cism in her voice as the two of them settled back
into the capacious seat and the chauffeur eased
away. 'Then what did he say about the breath-
lessness? The pain that I *know*, Papa, sometimes
strikes you in the chest?'

Her father waved an impatient hand. 'He's as
much of a fusspot as you are! Tells me to cut
down on work, lose some weight, take more exercise! As though I have time for any of that
nonsense!'

'Papa, he's a doctor—he knows what he's talking about,' Calanthe began.

She could feel anxiety beating up in her. For her father even to admit the doctor had told him to do anything at all about his lifestyle was not a good sign.

'He wants to do more tests! I gave him short shrift. I've agreed to take some pills, but nothing more! And you, my daughter, are not to fuss over me. I can't abide it!'

Abruptly, her father changed the subject.

'Is everything ready for lunch today with young Kavadis?'

Calanthe stiffened immediately. For two days she'd been trying not to think of the coming lunch. Trying not to think about what had happened at her father's birthday party at all.

So Nik had crawled out of the woodwork—after eight long years. Crawled out, so it seemed, as a wealthy man—a man important enough to be consulted by the Greek government on building earthquake-proof, environmentally sustainable, low-cost housing.

Well, what was that to her? Nothing! Nik was in her past. And he would never, *never* be allowed to invade her life again.

Except...

'You will be joining us for lunch, will you not, Calanthe?'

She started at her father's question. 'Me? No. Of course not.'

'Why not?' His tone was bland.

'It's a business lunch, Papa,' she answered tightly.

Her father ignored her objection. 'He's a very good-looking young man, is he not?' he observed, his voice blander still. 'And financially very sound. Well-respected too.' He paused. 'Not married either,' her father said, 'so I am informed.'

Calanthe's fingers clenched. 'Papa...' she said warningly.

But he would not be warned.

'Calanthe, my darling daughter, you know above all things I want your happiness! But the years are passing, and not just for me.' His voice changed, and something in it made her heart catch. 'Life does not last for ever, my dearest child. Your own mother was taken far too soon. As for me... Well, that quack just now has reminded me I am not immortal either—'

He broke off and Calanthe reached for his hands. Large and reassuring. The hands that had always protected her.

Even when I did not know I needed it...

Her thoughts swirled away. She knew just how much her father longed for her to marry, to choose one of the innumerable eligible potential husbands he had urged upon her. Knew

how he wanted her settled, married with chi
dren. Happy... In love with the man she marrie

But I've done love. And it tore me to shreds

Her father's hands pressed hers, then release
them with a pat.

'So,' he said, and his voice was bland agaim
'will you join us for lunch today, hmm? Your am
cient papa and the very handsome and eligibl
young Kyrios Kavadis?' He smiled. 'Look him
over,' he said. 'That's all I ask.'

Nikos stepped out of the hotel limo that ha
brought him to the Villa Petranakos in the up
market suburb of Kifissia and glanced up wit
an expression of appreciation as his architect
eye ran over it. These old mansions were wort
preserving, and this one had been sympathet
cally restored, he could see.

The grand front doors were thrown open an
Nikos strolled in, admiring the marbled inte
rior as much as the exterior. But he was not her
to admire an historic building. He was here fc
quite different reasons. A business associatio
with Georgios Petranakos was potentially valu
able. As the past had proved...

He slewed his mind away. Such barbed though
were not appropriate. His dark eyes veiled suc
denly. Even though they came full circle to th
present. To the other reason he was here today.

Will she be here too?

He couldn't call it. As the daughter of one of Greece's wealthiest men Calanthe would lead a hectic social life. She could be out and about right now…perhaps lunching with a lover—

The thought was a nail grating on a blackboard.

What did he know about her and the life she led now? Deliberately he had kept himself ignorant. Besides, he had had other things on his mind. Other priorities.

I made my choice at the time. Took the only choice that was right for me.

Took it? He had grabbed it with both hands.

He followed a manservant and was shown into a room opening off the spacious hall. Immediately, with a distinct kick to his pulse, he felt his eyes go straight to the woman standing by the window. Her stance was as stiff as it had been at her father's party, her face as expressionless. And every bit as exquisitely beautiful…

Her hair was confined into a knot at the nape of her neck. There were stud pearls at her ears and a simple pearl rope around her neck, their colour matching the pale silk jersey top she was wearing. Her slender waist was belted, and she wore a thin, calf-length A-line skirt in soft dove-grey that went with her low-heeled shoes.

She did not move. And even though she was

looking at him, she might as well have been made of marble.

Then his attention was called by her father, who was greeting him genially.

They took their places at the table. Nikos contented himself with merely nodding at Calanthe in a brief, civil gesture, murmuring a polite greeting, nothing more, and then looked across at his host as staff set the first course down, pouring wine and water for them all.

'I hope you will tell me something of the history of this most impressive mansion,' he said, with genuine appreciation in his voice. 'It has been superbly restored.'

His host smiled warmly, launching into the requisite account. Calanthe, Nikos saw from the outset, remained completely silent, merely eating and sipping water, her wine untouched. Tension radiated from her.

It did not deter him. He knew the reason for it. His gaze rested on her, veiled but measuring. He could hardly have expected a warm welcome from her, but that would not stop him.

Not now that I have seen her again.

He felt that kick in his pulse again…knew that he would not resist it. Would instead indulge it…

And why not? Now I move in her circles… now I am no longer that penniless architecture student earning money during my vacations by doing back-breaking labour on a construction site... I have every right to make a move.

Memory played in his head, enticing and alluring. From the very first moment she'd looked up at him, startled, from that dusty excavation trench, and he'd seen the tell-tale dilation of her pupils which her prickly, snobbish rebuff of him had not been able to give the lie to, he'd felt that kick—and from then on he'd known he'd wanted her. Oh, she'd tried to hold him off—those snide put-downs had been meant to deter him—but he'd brushed them aside, knowing why she was sniping at him.

For the same reason she was now attempting to freeze him out.

If she were not reacting to me as I am to her she would not bother freezing me out.

His lidded eyes perused her as he gave half an ear to what her father was saying about the restoration of the villa.

And if I were not reacting to her as I am then I would not be bothering to waste any time on her.

Thoughts played in his head. Eight years ago it had ended. But now...?

Now we could be good together—again...

He realised his host had moved on to another subject and switched his full attention back to him.

'You have soared high very swiftly,' Georgios was now saying to Nikos with approval. 'You are still a young man, but you have achieved a great deal for environmental sustainability with your innovative designs and construction methods.' A shrewd glance came Nikos's way. 'It was perceptive of you to patent your materials and your method for low-energy concrete production.'

Nikos nodded, taking a mouthful of the excellent wine that had been served with the meal. Calanthe, he noticed, was still not drinking hers.

Memory slid like a knife between his synapses.

That first night at the taverna—her knocking back the cheap local wine we were all drinking. The glow it brought to her eyes...the way she kept looking at me...could not take her eyes from me. How hard I had to work not to look only at her, as I wanted to...

He snapped the memory shut. Not now—not yet. There would be time for indulging in those memories. Maybe making new ones...

'Yes,' he answered his host. 'I saw no reason for others to benefit—perhaps those less responsibly-minded than I am determined to be. By patenting globally I can ensure they are used only in areas where it is environmentally appropriate. The continued use of concrete remains, of course, controversial, and is likely only to become increasingly so.'

His host addressed a technical question to him and Nikos followed his lead.

His eyes briefly encompassed Calanthe.

There is no animation in her face. She is beautiful—exquisitely so—but like a statue. Not flesh and blood.

Again, memory stabbed. More potent this time—much more potent.

Her head thrown back, her hair cascading over the pillows, ecstasy in her face...

With even more essential self-discipline, he snapped the memory shut. Returned to a discussion about reducing the energy requirements for making concrete and the commercial implications thereof.

His host's eyes rested speculatively on Nikos. 'Tell me, how long do you envisage being in Athens?'

'That will depend on how speedily the government officials decide to move during this consultation period,' Nikos replied drily.

'Hah, that means weeks!'

His host did not sound disapproving. Quite the reverse. He sat back, with an air of genial relaxation about him and a decided look of satisfaction in his face.

Then the maid and manservant were returning, clearing away the finished plates, serving a summer tart for dessert. As they disappeared Georgios Petranakos visibly changed gear, launching into expressing his views on the government ministers Nikos was likely to encounter during the consultation process.

Nikos paid attention—this was useful information to him—but the scrape of a chair made him turn his head. Calanthe was getting to her feet, depositing her linen napkin on the table.

'Papa, if you will excuse me? I'm not sure I have either the stamina, or indeed the interest, to cope with the ins and outs of politicians. I must be off.' She glanced down at Nikos. Gave a tight, unrevealing smile. 'Kyrios Kavadis.'

She nodded.

And took her leave.

Her low heels clicked on the marble floor. She was not even waiting for her father and his guest to get to their feet and was gone in seconds.

Calanthe headed up to the curving staircase as fast as she could without actually running, clutching at the banister. It had taken all her strength to endure lunch—to sit there while Nikos Kavadis talked to her father barely more than a metre from her across the table.

Her expression contorted. And, worse, her father was obviously pleased that he'd be hanging around Athens for weeks! And she knew why he was pleased...

She pulled her thoughts away from the temptation simply to tell her father just why Nikos

Kavadis was the very last man he should be encouraging in his endless matchmaking schemes. She felt her blood congeal at the thought of her father knowing…

She arrived at her bedroom and threw herself down on the bed, heart thudding. She wanted to pack…get out of Athens, get back to London. Get back to work. But her post at the museum was a job-sharing one, designed to give her time out here with her father and to put in some hours at one of the many Athenian museums on an exchange basis.

And now there was another reason to keep her in Greece. Calanthe felt an all too familiar anxiety biting at her. Her father might be playing down whatever it was his cardiologist had told him, but she could not dismiss it so easily. Her father was not well. So she could not run away just to get herself away from Nik.

She felt her hands claw into the bed-covering.

I have to tough this out. I have to! He'll be here a while and then he'll go. Disappear again like he did before. But this time he'll disappear with my blessing—with my abject relief!

If she could just hold out till then…

Then it would be over.

Like it had been before.

It was the only hope she could cling to.

CHAPTER THREE

NIKOS CLIMBED INTO the hotel limo that was co lecting him from the Petranakos mansion, hi mood excellent for several reasons. Firstly, b cause he'd gained useful information abou the politicians he was going to be dealing wit here. And secondly, his host had more than on mentioned his latest birthday—a milestone tha might make a man think seriously about step ping back from business, slowing the pace. Co sider passing the burden on to young shoulders.

The words had been accompanied by a na rowed look directed at his guest. An assessin look… A speculative one…

Nikos might have made nothing of it, or li tle enough, except for the reaction of the oth person present at the lunch. From his place the foot of the table Nikos had heard Calanthe knife and fork clatter to the plate. And then wh surely had been an intake of breath that had be stifled as soon as it had been drawn.

Which could only mean...

The expression in his dark eyes was speculative...

Yes, precisely *what* could that mean?

Well, that was speculation and inward reflection for another time. For now it was time to focus on the third and most satisfying reason for his good mood.

Encountering Calanthe once more was proving as fortuitous as it had eight years ago. Seeing her again had brought that time vividly to his mind again. Eight years ago she had crossed his path and shared with him delights that had been memorable in his youth. Memorable, indeed...

His expression flickered.

It had been a golden summer in the weeks he'd spent with her at the excavation. A 'golden treasure' he had called her—and so she had proved.

Something changed in his eyes...hardened. Then he frowned. That was not why he'd called her his golden treasure. That had been because she herself had been such a find!

I discovered her when I had no thought of doing so—no thought of anything that summer but hard work and putting aside money for my tuition fees.

Then Calanthe—lovely, ardent and so, so giving—had appeared in his life and he had not been able to resist her...

Nor she him.

Once he had won her over she had given herself unstintingly and he had reciprocated—treasuring the gift she had given him, celebrating, with her, the transition from maiden to woman as she had trusted him to be her first lover.

His expression shadowed suddenly.

She trusted me with her body but with nothing else. Not with who she really was...

He pushed the thought aside. Not wanting to think about why she had proved such a golden treasure.

That didn't matter—not any more. All that mattered was how they had been together, he and Calanthe, that summer long ago, in each other's arms, passionate and carefree.

His expression changed again, became a frown again, but with a different cause. He was questioning himself.

Just what had been so good about those weeks with her before they had come to the end? Once she had stopped holding him at bay, accepted what was happening between them, she'd relaxed with him completely—and he with her. He'd singled her out, sitting beside her at the taverna in the evenings, interesting himself in her part of the dig. Interesting himself in her completely.

Her ready laugh, her warmth... I could not

keep my eyes from her, and nor could she keep hers from me.

The other students had accepted what was happening—had treated them as a couple.

And that is what we became.

He'd revelled in the ardour of her lovemaking, the glow in her eyes. He had dedicated his time to her, had eyes for no other woman but her...

Reminiscence filled him and a frown plucked at his brows. Eight years had passed since he'd last seen her, but had there ever been anyone like her in his life? Women had always come easily to him, even when he was a penniless student. Now... His expression grew cynical. Now, of course, he thought caustically, he could have just about any woman he cast his eyes at. Except—

The frown deepened. Still he was questioning himself. There had been other attractive girls on that dig, but none had existed for him except for Calanthe. He tried to call up the images of any of the women he'd consorted with from time to time in his non-stop climb to fortune but none came to mind. Not any more—not since he'd seen Calanthe again.

In only a few days, out of nowhere, having never expected to see her again, he found she had totally imprinted herself on his conscious-ness.

She is dominating my thoughts....my desires...

The frown cleared from his face. That was hardly a problem—only a challenge.

A challenge he would meet gladly.

Determinedly.

Oh, she could freeze him out all she liked, but he knew better than to think he could not *un*freeze her. Reclaim the ardent, eager lover he had known, who had given herself so rapturously to him and would once more.

He was certain of it.

He settled back more comfortably into the deep leather car seat.

The only question was how and when to make his next move.

Calanthe set her coffee cup back on the tray, nestling back against her pillows. She was indulging in breakfast in bed, having been out late the night before. And the night before that. She was keeping busy—very busy—socialising to the hilt. Far more than she usually did when she was in Athens with her father.

Last night she'd been out to dinner with Yannis, one of her regular 'swains', as she wryly called the well-heeled young men who moved in her father's elite circles and would happily be a lot more to her than a mere dinner date if she ever showed the slightest inclination.

Her father, as she knew all too well, kept on

ping that one day she would choose one of
em to marry. He made no secret of it. And as
ne had gone by she had come to accept that
e day, eventually—though not yet!—she prob-
ly would accept a proposal from Yannis, or
meone like him. Someone who was easy-go-
g, pleasant company…who would make a loyal
sband and an affectionate father to whatever
ildren they might have.

Such a marriage—a marriage in which burn-
g passion and heady desire played no role—
as what she had come to reconcile herself to.
had come to seem…acceptable.

Except—

She pulled her thoughts away as emotion
led her—emotion that she did not want, that
e deplored, rejected. No, she must *not* go down
at dangerous path. Only one man had ever set
er passion on fire… Made her ache with de-
re for him…

A man she must guard herself against with
l her strength.

And he had walked back into her life again.

Bleakly, she stared unseeingly into her bed-
om, feeling a restlessness seize her that had
right to be there.

For her father's sake she was stuck here in
thens, not wanting to abandon him while she
ill had cause to worry over his ill health, deny

it as he insisted on doing. And Nikos was here too. She knew that because her father kept her informed of it. She'd dreaded this last week, lest her father take it into his head to matchmake again and invite Nikos for dinner. But she'd been blessedly spared that ordeal. Even more blessedly, Nikos had not attempted to get in touch with her.

Maybe I have nothing to fear after all! Maybe he really is only interested in a business acquaintance with my father! It would be useful enough to him, after all.

Her mouth twisted. Yes, her father's use to Nikos was attested…

Again, she pulled her thoughts away. She would not think of Nikos Kavadis—would not pay attention to the restlessness inside her. She would think, instead, of what she would do today.

She might head into central Athens…put in some time at the museum where she did some exchange work for her London museum during her long stays in Greece visiting her father.

Or perhaps one of her friends might suggest lunch somewhere—maybe down on the Athenian Riviera at Glyfada…or they could take a boat from Piraeus out to one of the offshore islands and make a day of it.

Even as she mulled over these possibilities

the house phone on her bedside table rang. She picked it up, expecting it to be one of her friends—or Yannis, perhaps, thanking her for the evening before and suggesting another outing today.

But it was none of them. It was Nikos.

He had caught her off guard. He knew it the moment he spoke, by the sudden intake of breath at the other end of the line. Well, he wanted her off-guard—that was why he'd left it nearly a week before making contact with her.

OK, so he'd been full-on anyway, immersed in initial meetings with government officials as well as a whole slew of business meetings on his own account—including with Georgios Petrana-kos—which he was using his time in Athens to make the most of. But now he'd cleared his desk and another priority had taken over. The one he was focussing on today.

'Come to lunch,' he said, making no bones about it.

'I'm otherwise engaged,' came the immediate stiff reply.

'Your housekeeper says not,' Nikos riposted. 'I was thinking,' he went on, 'of a leisurely jaunt out of the city. How about we go to Sounion? Take a picnic?' He paused deliberately. 'Your father thinks you've been burning the candle at

both ends. He's suggested you need to slow t
pace. With me.'

He could hear only silence on the line. I
didn't let it last more than a microsecond, b
fore speaking again.

'Good, that's settled. I'll pick you up at ha
twelve.'

Then he rang off, a smile of satisfaction pla
ing about his lips.

She could have kept to her room. Cited a hea
ache—a hangover, even! Could have phon
her father at his office and rung a peal over h
head for setting her up, as he so obviously ha
Could have ripped into Elena the housekeep
for blabbing.

There were half a dozen things Calanthe kne
she could have done—but she hadn't.

And she knew perfectly well why.

There were things that needed to be ma
clear.

Crystal-clear.

She emerged at the time Nikos had said to fi
him waiting in a low-slung, silver-grey, ope
topped car sporting an Italian crest on its lo
bonnet. His own, or hired? She didn't know, a
didn't care.

He leant across to open the passenger door f
her, nodding a greeting as he did so, which s

did not return. She had nothing civil to say to him. She slipped into the passenger seat, smoothing her pale green palazzo pants which she wore with their matching top. Like her, Nikos was wearing sunglasses, and she was glad of it. Perhaps they need never actually look at each other for the duration.

She sat back, pulling the seat belt across herself, burningly conscious of his presence beside her. Though she did not look at him she'd taken in that he was casually dressed in an open-necked shirt, cuffs turned back, his dark hair—so much shorter now than it had been that long-ago summer—slightly ruffled by the breeze. She felt her stomach clench as she caught the faint scent of aftershave.

Doggedly, she stared ahead, not letting herself look at him as he drove the car down the drive and turned out onto the highway, keeping deliberately silent. This was not a social outing—she did not even owe him courtesy.

Her face was set, more stony than ever.

He didn't speak either—only took the direction to Cape Sounion on the south-east of the Attica Peninsula, guiding the powerful car through the busy traffic until he could open the throttle clear of the city.

She was glad they were going to Sounion. It would be sufficiently out of the way for what she intended. Deliberately, she breathed slowly and evenly, refusing to let her tension show.

But she was as taut as a high-tension cable and she knew it. Did Nikos know it as well? If he did, he'd know why.

And I want him to know—I damn well want him to know!

Emotion rose in her. Emotion that had been suppressed for so long now that she might have thought it extinct. But it was no more extinct than the volcano on Thera had been extinct. It seethed like boiling magma, just below the rigidly composed air with which she sat so motionless beside Nikos.

He was so close…

Ripples like earth tremors vibrated within her. All she had to do was lift her hand to touch him…

Instead, she sat quite still, hands folded in her lap, gazing out through the windscreen, her expression impassive. Saying nothing. But feeling so much…

'What about here? It catches the breeze and the view is spectacular!'

Nikos's tone was inviting—deliberately so. He'd studiously ignored Calanthe's silence on the way here. It was, after all, to be expected. And he knew why.

She's spoiling for a fight.

That, he knew, was why she'd accepted his invitation. Why she was having anything to do with him. Why, indeed, he'd suggested driving out to Cape Sounion—way out of the city—taking with them the lavish picnic his hotel's kitchens had supplied him with, and which he now proceeded to unload from the small boot of the car.

It was a hire car, but he'd chosen and driven it with pleasure—even though the presence of Calanthe at his side, stony-faced and silent, had been a distraction from putting the car through its paces.

Closing the boot with a snap, he led the way to a picnic spot with panoramic views over the Cape and the Aegean Sea beyond. He spread out the blanket then hunkered down to open up the cool box, extracting a chilled bottle of white wine and one of sparkling water.

'Wine, water, or a spritzer?' he enquired genially.

'Water,' came the terse reply from Calanthe.

She was sitting herself down, carefully angling her legs away from him and keeping a good metre distant, towards the edge of the blanket. She did not remove her dark glasses, and neither did he take off his own. After all, the sun sparkling over the blue water beyond the cliff-edge was very bright. That was excuse enough.

The real reason, though, as Nikos well knew, was to give herself a sense of protection.

He carefully poured the chilled sparkling water into one of the glasses provided and handed it to her. She took it, scrupulously avoiding the slightest chance of their fingers brushing, and drank from its contents gracefully. Nikos mixed himself a spritzer and raised his glass.

'What shall we drink to?' he asked. His tone was deliberately bland.

He saw her lovely mouth tighten, her fingers around the glass do likewise.

'To never seeing each other again. *Again.*'

She knocked back another big mouthful of her water, difficult when it was effervescing so frenziedly in the heat, but the gesture served its purpose. As did her words.

The opening salvo.

Had she not been wearing her shades, Nikos knew she'd be glaring at him with a killing basilisk gaze. But his only response was to take up a deliberately relaxed pose, stretching out his legs, crossing them at the ankles and leaning back on his elbow.

Yet behind the relaxed pose he was bracing himself.

The only accusation she can throw at me is that I left her. Nothing else.

He had made sure of that—made it a condition to her father's fixers.

And all that's in the past—long gone.

So there was no point dwelling on it, was there? It was the present he was concerned with now. Only the present.

I am not concerned that our affair ended—or why. I am only concerned with what I want there to be between us now.

His eyes rested on her. Even with that net of tension over her, radiating her resistance and hostility towards him, she was still so beautiful it could take his breath away. He wanted to cast his gaze on her, drink her in… And then reach for her…feel her resistance to him melting away, feel her mouth opening to his, her arms coming around him, her body yielding to his… warm and ardent and eager…

Memories, delectable and enticing, were like tendrils in his mind, but he pushed them away. He was not there yet…

'Why?' he said, tilting his head to look directly at her, answering her with a tone of voice that was neither challenging nor countering, only inquiring. He was keeping his cool. Surely the best way to handle this.

He could see her expression change.

'*Why?*' she repeated.

It was like a bullet. Shot from her. Right at him.

She reared back. 'You have the almighty *nerve* to sit there and ask *why*!'

More bullets, spitting at him like machine gun fire.

'You think—you *really* think—that you can just, oh, so casually invite me out! Behave as though *nothing* had happened between us! As if—'

He cut across her. 'It did happen, Calanthe. Our time together that summer. And even if it hadn't...'

He changed his voice, his gaze never leaving hers. He wanted her to understand that she could protest all she liked but it would make no difference.

'Even if the very first time I'd ever set eyes on you had been at your father's birthday party I would still have asked you out. Still have wanted you here. Because...' his voice became a caress '...you are simply the most beautiful woman I have ever set eyes on.'

He saw her face work. 'Don't. Just...*don't*.'

Her words were not bullets now, but tight, like wire pulled to breaking strain.

He gave a shrug. 'Why not? Why not tell you

the truth? You were irresistible eight years ago and you are even more so now.'

She shot forward, fury in the set of her shoulders.

'Oh, so damn irresistible that you walked out on me without a word! Walked out and—'

She broke off, twisting her head away, knocking back another gulp of water and then setting the glass down. He saw her take a breath, a deliberate one, to steady herself. Then she whipped her head back round. Returned to the attack.

But he did not let her speak. There was only one way he could answer her, only one response he could make. Anything else was out of the question.

She must never know why I left her.

Not that what he was going to say to her was not the truth. He felt a flicker of emotion rise within him. It was just not *all* the truth...

'Calanthe, what we had together was good—memorably so! But,' he said, holding her unseen gaze, 'it was a summer romance. Wonderful while it lasted—but...' He paused, knowing he had to say this. 'Then it ended—just as the summer ended.'

He was speaking carefully. He knew that he was doing so, and knew why he was doing so. He was keeping to what he could say...explain.

To continue his defence, at least where

he could, he went on, 'And, to set the recor
straight, I did not leave *"without a word"*. I to
Georgia that I'd been unexpectedly called awa
and I left you a note. I'm sorry not to have to
you in person, but I had to leave the island rig
away.'

He'd had no choice—her father's fixers ha
made that crystal-clear to him. No more contac

*Not that I could have looked her in the fac
again...*

His mind pulled away. Those memories we
too jarring. Emotion rose in him again. And b
sides, he'd had another pressing reason for lea
ing the island immediately...

'Why?' Her blunt question was still hosti
'Just what was so pressing...so urgent?'

She was staring at him, her face immobil
He found himself wishing she was not wearir
dark glasses, so he could see the expression
her eyes. See what she was thinking. He'd a
ways been able to see what she was feeling.
she'd never hidden her emotions from him...

His mouth tightened. No, she'd never dor
that, all right! But they'd been feelings that ha
only...complicated things.

And now—now he wanted things to be sir
ple between them.

He wanted to put aside those elements of t

past that jarred, whose memory was unwelcome—not let them get in the way now.

Because what I want now is the present—only the present.

His eyes washed over her again from behind the protection of his shades. And that was so very, very enticing...

Again he felt desire rise through him. The impact she'd had on him all those years ago was stronger now, so much stronger...

His own words that he'd spoken just now hung in his head—irrefutable and compelling.

'You are the most beautiful woman I have ever set eyes on.'

But he could not yet indulge himself. He still had to dispose of her anger to him. Get it out of the way. Explain—justify—his behaviour in the only way he could.

Her hidden gaze was still levelled at him. Her fingers still tight around her glass. Her body was still quite immobile. Tense.

'Family matters,' he replied. 'My grandmother...'

He left it at that. The only way he could leave it.

He saw her mouth thin, as if he'd uttered a typical self-exonerating excuse. He didn't want to hear her put that into words, so he took control of the moment instead.

'Calanthe, I know that the way we ended eight years ago upset you, but... Well, like I said, what we had was a summer romance. It was always going to end... You went back to your life.'

His voice hardened unconsciously. After all, her life—her *real* life—had not been what she'd let him think. She had not been just another one of the bunch of British university students on a working holiday in Greece.

He continued, 'And I went back to mine. We went our separate ways.'

She was still keeping that hidden gaze levelled at him, immobile and tense.

He levered himself forward, looked directly at her. Said now what he wanted to say. What he wanted her to hear. What he had brought her here to say.

'But now I'm back.'

CHAPTER FOUR

CALANTHE STARED AT HIM.

'But now I'm back.'

His words, so coolly uttered, stung like wasp stings on her bare arms. She felt emotion rise in her like boiling magma. But somehow she kept a lid on it. She was no longer that nineteen-year-old in the throes of agonising first love. She was a mature woman. Calm, composed, under control.

My own control.

'Back for what, Nik?' she asked.

Her voice was dry. As dry as sand.

She was aware far too late that she'd called him by the name she'd used eight years ago.

He smiled. It was a smile that reached back through the years. A smile she had not seen directed at her for those eight long years that divided them. A smile that divided her stupid, foolish ingenue self from the mature, capable, self-controlled woman she was now.

'For you, of course, Calanthe,' he said.

For a second—an endless, motionless second—the words hung in the air between them. Both of them looked at each other, their gazes veiled from the other.

Then he broke the moment. Set down his spritzer and leaned forward to examine the rest of the contents of the picnic box.

'I'm hungry,' he announced. 'Let's eat.'

She watched him busy himself extracting carefully wrapped parcels from the box, setting them out on the blanket, before peeling off the wrappings. Her mind was in turmoil. She wanted to yell at him, shout at him, throw everything she had buried so deep within her those long eight years ago when he had walked out on her...everything that had festered and burned and *hurt* so much...

And more than hurt.

Worse than hurt.

Once again, as she had the night after her father's birthday party, when she had lain sleepless in her bed, with Nik having just walked into her life again as he had, she felt the hot, humid drenching of humiliation rise up in her unbearably. She forced it from her. Refusing to give it entry.

Her expression hardened as she went on watching him unpack the picnic. Her mouth

visted. So Nik—rich and successful now—
ought he could just move in on her again!
hought he could stroll into her life, driving his
ncy car, staying in Athens' best hotel, flashing
is cash around as casually as if it were candy.
hought he could just stroll right up to her and
ke up with her again!

He really thought that?

After what he'd done to her?

*Well, he can think again! Because it will never,
ever happen.*

She was safe from him. Had made herself
)—painstakingly, painfully, assiduously and
eterminedly—with every year that separated
er from that long-ago summer when she had
een so vulnerable to him, so trusting...

He can't get to me again. Not now.

Because now, as the bitter taste in her mouth
ccentuated, she knew what kind of man he was.
What he was prepared to stoop to...

A 'summer romance'. That was what he was
ılling what they'd had. Even though, for her, it
ıd been so much more than that.

She felt her heart clench.

*I really thought myself in love—I truly, truly
id...*

The pain inside her twisted, wrenching at her
notions.

He looked me in the face and told me it was

just a summer romance. That that was the only reason he ended it.

But she knew better. Bitterly, bitterly so.

Again, the memory of her father's words to her as she'd sobbed her youthful heartbreak sounded in her head, telling her just what the man who'd romanced her all summer had done... what kind of man it had proved him to be.

And he thinks I don't know. It's obvious he thinks that.

Well, she would not enlighten him. Let him trot out whatever he liked about 'summer romance'!

Because I can't bear to tell him that I know—I can't bear to feel again, in front of him, the humiliation of it...

She screwed her eyes shut behind her dark glasses, grateful for them, schooling her emotions back under her control. She would not let them out again. Instead, she would deal with the situation as it presented itself. Behave as though he meant nothing to her. Because that would be the least painful to her, and protecting herself was her priority.

She took a silent breath, opened her eyes again, and watched him finish the unpacking, her expression impassive, making her features relax. She was safe from him—whatever he might so shamelessly, arrogantly think. That was what she had to hang on to.

He sat back, glancing up at her, and smiled. 'OK, what do you want to start with? It all looks good! There's seafood salad, chicken breast with some kind of dressing, Parma ham and smoked salmon—and any number of side salads!'

He indicated the spread with a sweep of his hand. His tone was genial, amicable, easy-going, his smile warm.

Out of nowhere, memory hit. She'd picnicked with Nik before, during their lunch breaks at the excavation, though nothing like this grand gourmet feast. They'd bought *gyros* at the harbour-side, clambered up the narrow goats' path to look down over the azure sea, settling themselves down.

Nik had smiled at her… Just as he was smiling now.

The pain was visceral, like a blow to her lungs. She forced it away. Forced the memory away. Forced away all memories of Nik from that time so many years ago. She would not give them oxygen to flare and burn her. Instead she dragged her eyes down to the repast spread on the dry ground. Against her volition she suddenly felt hungry. Breakfast had been a long time ago. Would it really kill her to eat some of this picnic?

She reached for one of the plates, hoverir
her fork over several of the dishes, then takir
a little of each. She was hungry—she would e:
And the fact that she was doing so in the pre
ence of the man she had never wanted to s
again in her life she would completely ignor
with strength of will and absolute self-contro

I won't let him get to me. I can't and I won'

Yet even as her eyes rested on him, still bles
edly veiled by her dark glasses, and she sat bac
making her position more comfortable and for
ing into the delicious food, she felt sensatic
sweep over her.

Nik at twenty-five had been a hunk of the fir
order—she hadn't needed Georgia's breathle
admiration to tell her that. She'd had eyes
her head. Eyes that had wanted to do as she h
done that first fateful night at the taverna: sin
ply gaze and gaze and gaze…

As they still did.

She felt something squeeze inside her—som
thing catch. Her gaze rested on him now as hel
lessly as it had eight long years ago.

He's matured. That raw, rough toughness h
matured into a lean strength. Smoothed itse
Honed itself. Then, he looked exactly what l
was—a man in his mid-twenties, muscles pumpe
from hard physical labour, hair over-long, jawli
roughened, hands callused. But now…

Now the years sat on him well, as did his wealth. He might be lounging back on the cliffs of Cape Sounion, but there was a sophistication to him now, a cosmopolitan air that went with the expensive casual clothes, the impeccably groomed hair, the pristine jawline.

She felt again that tightening, that catching of something inside her. Eight years had passed, but one truth still forced itself upon her—however unwilling she was to hear it, however much she might bitterly resist it and resent it.

In her head, his words echoed.

'You were irresistible eight years ago, and you are even more so now.'

And, with a heaviness that seemed to crush her like a weight she could no longer bear, she knew that those words were true of her feelings too.

And the knowledge was unendurable.

Somehow she got through the rest of the picnic. For reasons she did not want to think about—because it was somehow easier on her not to do so...because letting Nikos know how hideously he'd hurt her was just too painful—she let Nikos behave as though this were just a normal occasion. As if he really was just a new business acquaintance of her father, inviting his daughter for this al fresco outing.

That, she knew, with a shiver of coldness, would, in fact, be what her father would assume.

That I'm going out on a date with a new man. A man who, so far, has passed my father's eligibility test.

The cold pool in the pit of her stomach chilled even more. If her father only knew—

She cut off her thoughts. No point giving room to them. No point doing anything but what she was doing now: having the semblance of a civil, social picnic with a man who was all but a stranger, who had obviously invited her out because she was Georgios Petranakos's very attractive daughter.

And his heiress.

The word tolled in her brain. With all its implications.

She shook them from her. They were irrelevant. Nikos Kavadis would not even get to first base with her, let alone meet whatever aspirations he might be contemplating giving house room to.

But what, exactly, was he after?

She felt the question in her head…felt herself shy away from it. Eight years ago he'd romanced her, not knowing whose daughter she was.

Now he did.

Again, her thoughts pulled away.

No, above all, she mustn't go there.

He was peeling a peach, then cutting it for her, offering her a slice. Carefully, she took the succulent fruit and slipped it into her mouth. There had been something unnervingly intimate in the way Nikos had offered it to her.

She swallowed it down, then reached for her water, nearly finishing it off. She poured the rest over fingers that were sticky from the peach. Then she got to her feet.

'I haven't been to Sounion for a while—I might as well see the temple up close now I'm here,' she announced.

She kept her tone cool…impersonal.

Nikos stood up too.

'Do you want to stay for the sunset?' he asked. 'If so, I'm sure we can get a coffee at one of the hotels by the beach to while away the time.'

Calanthe shook her head. It was hours till sunset—the famous 'show' that tourists came to see, watching as it set behind the ancient ruins of the temple starkly outlined on the promontory.

'I'm going out this evening,' she said. 'I don't want to be back too late.'

'Who's the lucky man?' Nikos's enquiry was casual as he stooped to pack away the picnic things.

'A girlfriend,' Calanthe answered without thinking. Then she was cross that she hadn't said her evening out was to be with a man. 'A concert,' she added for good measure. 'Schubert.'

She watched as Nikos swung up the picnic box. Another memory darted into Calanthe's head—how he'd so effortlessly hefted a sack of dry cement into a waiting wheelbarrow on the construction site next to the dig. Georgia's eyes had gone to the ripped torso on display as he had done so and she'd given a sigh.

'Oh, for your looks, Cal!' she'd said. *'He only has eyes for you, you know.'*

Her expression changed. Hardened. In her head she heard again his declaration—that he had come back.

For her.

She felt a shiver go through her. A shiver that should not be there. Yet there it was, all the same. A shiver of awareness...of vulnerability.

Nik—back in my life. Wanting me again.

She felt the power of his declaration—the declaration he'd so shamelessly, arrogantly made to her—and yet for all his shamelessness and arrogance she could feel its power....

He held out a hand as if to guide her as they headed back to the car. She ignored it. That was the only sane thing to do. Ignore it. Ignore everything about him. Shut him out.

I've said what I came here to say. Made it

rystal-clear that I want absolutely nothing to 'o with him, ever again!

And now she needn't.

That was all she must hang on to. Anything lse was far too dangerous.

Earth-shaker.' Nikos stood contemplating the uins of the ancient temple to the powerful sea god Poseidon, brother of Zeus, patron of all sea-arers.

Calanthe spoke at his side. '*Enosichthon*— hat's what Homer calls him. Though there are variants on that.'

She was speaking civilly to him—that was something at least, Nikos allowed, bringing his gaze back to her. He was taking it carefully. She'd had her showdown with him—the one he'd braced himself for, knowing he needed to get it out of the way. Defuse the past so he could move on to the future.

His eyes rested on her. Every glance at her only confirmed what he wanted. No matter how they'd parted eight years ago—or *why* they'd parted—right now he wanted only the immediate future with her.

He heard his own words to her echo in his head.

'You were irresistible eight years ago and you are even more so now.'

Nothing had ever been truer. She had swept him away—then and now.

He realised she was speaking again, and made himself pay attention to what she was saying.

'It's strange,' she mused, 'that a sea god should also be a god of earthquakes.'

'Well, we think of earthquakes as being of the land, but they're caused by the movement of the crust's tectonic plates, and many tectonic fault lines lie underwater or along coastlines,' Nikos explained. 'Greece is very vulnerable, sitting in the midst of some very complex plate boundaries. The whole area is moving and jolting as the plates grind together—hence the frequent earthquakes, some minor and some devastating, like the one that caught my parents—' He stopped.

Calanthe looked at him. He looked away. He should not have mentioned his parents, but it was too late now.

'They were killed in an earthquake when I was five,' he said.

He heard the intake of her breath.

'Nik... I didn't know. You never... You never mentioned that when we first—'

She broke off.

He looked at her, his expression veiled.

'There was quite a lot that didn't get mentioned,' he replied.

He shifted restlessly. There were things that

perhaps they should have known about each other then. And things that should never be known...even now.

Especially now...

He walked a little way away, feeling the afternoon heat beating down. The blue of the sea was azure, brilliant in the sun, and the ceaseless chorus of cicadas was all around. He had touched on a dangerous subject and wanted to move away from it.

'They put the temple here because it was the first glimpse of Attica for ships sailing home, didn't they?' he heard himself say, gazing around, wanting something totally neutral to say. 'Presumably by the time they could see the temple they were all but home and dry.'

'Seafaring was a dangerous business in those days,' she answered.

'Yet it was undertaken so much, all the same. All that trade constantly going on...taking goods back and forth across the Aegean and further. I remember from the dig that—'

He stopped again.

There was a pause. But then Calanthe picked up the thread, her tone of voice unexceptional.

'Yes, that was what pleased Prof so much— that the pots we dug up proved that trade with Corinth, even in that difficult era, had not disappeared.'

'What happened to all the finds?'

Nikos made sure his voice was simply civ illy enquiring, glad that he could do so and th. she could reply in kind. He wanted to be abl to have a simple, normal conversation with he not something charged with stressful emotion

Like fault lines between us, creating tensio I do not want.

She was answering his question, her voice a civil as his.

'After cataloguing and so on they ended up i the local museum. A couple of the more impo tant pieces went to Corinth, I think.'

She wandered off, her attention apparentl taken by the impressive row of columns marcl ing along the flanks of the temple ruins. Nik strolled after her, placing the palm of his har on one of the fluted columns experimentally.

'The marble is quite coarse-grained,' he i formed her, wanting to keep this normal conve sation going. 'As you'll know, the current temp is built on the ruins of an older, Archaic peri temple, which was made of limestone. The tw have been very skilfully integrated.'

He pointed out areas where it was possible discern, with a trained eye, what he meant, a saw that she was listening. It called to his mir how she'd listened at that first taverna meal a those years ago, as he'd discoursed on building methods in the ancient world.

Was that what made me want to make her think differently about me? Make her want to want me?

He looked covertly at her now. Her whole appearance was so different from what it had been eight years ago, when she was a teenager. Her outfit alone—from some pricey boutique in Kolonaki, no doubt—and her chic, poised elegance were a world away from the way she'd looked back then.

Like she was just one of those run-of-the-mill students... Not even letting on she was half-Greek. Let alone whose daughter she was.

That was definitely one of the things that had never got mentioned...

He felt emotion twist in him. Pushed it aside. He didn't want the past making things complicated now, in the present. He'd called their affair a summer romance—and that was what it had had to be.

But now...?

Now I'm part of her world.

It had taken long studies, non-stop hard work and taking risks, unsure if they'd pay off. But they had—more than handsomely. And now he was reaping the rewards. He gave a silent nod to himself. He was doing some good in the world as well.

As if she'd caught his thoughts, Calanthe spoke. Her voice was different, somehow, from her impersonal conversational tone as they'd explored the temple ruins.

'What you told me just now… I didn't know about the earthquake in your childhood. That's why you specialise in earthquake-proof housing, isn't it, Nik?'

Her question was softly spoken, and for the first time since their paths had crossed again there was sympathy in it.

'Because of your parents.' She paused, a slight frown forming. 'What happened to you after… after your parents were killed?'

'I went to live with my maternal grandmother,' he answered. 'She…she was very important to me.'

He stopped. This was dangerous territory again.

Abruptly, he glanced at his watch. Changed the subject just as abruptly.

'If you're going out tonight I'd better run you back. I haven't forgotten how vicious the Athens traffic is.'

He headed back down towards the car park and Calanthe followed him. As he walked he put the past behind him. His parents were long gone, his grandmother had died three years ago—he felt emotion stab at him for a moment—and his youthful romance with Calanthe had come to the end it had. For the reasons it had had to…

But those reasons no longer stand in the way. That is what I welcome. So the way ahead with her is clear.

All he had to do was convince her of that. And he would, too.

His gaze went sideways to Calanthe. Even at the end of a hot day outdoors she still looked cool and elegant. And so breathtakingly beautiful!

One thing was certain, however many years had passed. And his own words to her over lunch echoed in his head.

'You were the most beautiful woman I'd ever set eyes on.'

And she still was. As irresistible now as she had been then…

CHAPTER FIVE

CALANTHE LEANT ON the ferry's railings, gazing back at the port of Piraeus as it receded into the distance, the churning wake of the ferry showing its path. She was glad to be out of Athens, even if only for the weekend. She was heading for an island villa belonging to a friend who was throwing a lavish party.

Most of the guests were being flown out there, or would arrive in private yachts. Calanthe, however, was taking the public ferry quite deliberately. She lived in two worlds and always had. Her mother's middle-class world of taking public transport and her father's wealthy VIP world of limos, yachts and helicopters.

She'd always moved easily between the two, depending on whether she was in the UK or in Athens. The only exception had been that fateful dig during her student days, when she had brought her UK self to Greece for the summer.

No wonder Nikos didn't have any idea about hose daughter I was.

And she'd wanted to keep it that way. Hadn't anted her father's wealth impacting on what 1e'd had with Nik that glorious summer. Com- icating things...

Painful emotion plucked at her she watched raeus recede across the widening gap of sea, :r mind going yet again to their picnic at Cape)union. Her expression hardened. Nikos had aimed that what had been between them had :en nothing more than a summer romance. ever intended to last. And that that was why it 1d ended the way it had.

She felt herself waver. Almost...*almost*...she)uld believe him.

Her mouth twisted.

Except that she knew otherwise. Bitterly, sav- ;ely knew otherwise...

Restlessly, she moved away from the rail, :ading for a seating area. Had she been wise to) to Sounion with Nik? Yes, she'd been able to t rip at him, make it clear she wanted nothing ore to do with him. But just seeing him, spend- g time in his company, however tense, had ade her ultra-aware of him all over again—of s sheer masculinity, of how strong the mag- :tism was that he somehow exerted over her.

And she'd been made aware of more than that.

Made aware of that pang of sympathy that had smote her as he'd told her about the sad fate of his parents. She'd seen him as a little boy, bereft and orphaned, being taken in by his grandmother to grow up with her.

She pulled her thoughts away. She didn't want to think of Nikos like that. Deserving her sympathy. It was as if she was letting her guard down about him, and she could not risk that. Could not risk it at all.

Since that day at Sounion she'd come to terms with Nik's return to Greece. Had decided she would put the past behind her, but would not let Nik back into her life. That would be an act of insanity...

Had he accepted that whatever it was he wanted of her now—all that he had said to her at Sounion—was impossible? Perhaps he had. It was over ten days since then, and he'd made no attempt to see her again or ask her out.

She was relieved—of course she was. What else should she be? No other emotion was permissible. Her father, too, had said nothing, and she was relieved at that, too. She did not want him thinking of Nik as any possible kind of suitor.

I don't want to have to tell him who Nik is— who he once was. He's clearly made no connection, and I don't want him to.

No, the past had to stay in the past. That was the only way she could cope with the present.

And the only way I can cope with having seen Nik again is by not seeing him!

That was the safest way. To wait it out until he left Athens and she was safe from the danger of running into him again. It was her major reason for looking forward to the coming weekend villa party—it would get her out of the city…help get Nik out of her head.

Determinedly, she sat herself down on one of the benches on the cooler, more shady side of the deck, extracting from her bag one of the specialist art history journals she subscribed to, intending to while away the ferry crossing.

She had barely opened it when a shadow fell over her. She glanced up.

Froze.

It was Nik.

Shock was stark in her face. Nik saw it instantly. More than shock. Dismay. And something more than that. The flash in her eyes told him that all her anger, all her rejection of him, all her scathing repudiation, all her blanking of him…all of that was a lie.

He felt a tight, justified stab of satisfaction.

He sat down opposite her.

'What the *hell*,' she spat at him, 'are you doi
here?'

He crossed one leg over the other in a le
surely, relaxed fashion.

'The same as you are. Heading for the V
lous party.'

'You don't know Marina Volous!'

'No, I know her husband. A business assoc
ation… He's in finance, as I'm sure you kno
and a useful contact. He invited me. Tell n
something…' his tone changed '…why are yc
travelling on the public ferry and not taking or
of the private transfers laid on for guests?'

There was an edge in his voice—he cou
hear it. Knew why it was there.

'Do you enjoy play-acting that you're just a
ordinary member of the public? The way yc
pretended when you were a student on that dig

He saw her face tighten.

'There was no pretence, Nikos. And, althoug
it's absolutely none of your business, my Engli
mother—as you may recall me telling you th
summer—raised me on her own, and always i
sisted I should be able to live without relying c
my father. She earned her own living—she w
a hairdresser and beautician—and apart fro
visits to Greece during school holidays I liv
a perfectly ordinary life. Not poor, but not ri

either. My father paid for my university course, but that was all.'

His expression was sceptical. 'She wasn't a wealthy divorcee?' he challenged.

'She wasn't a divorcee at all!' came the riposte. 'She never married my father—she didn't want to. Her choice, not his. She didn't want to be tied down in marriage. But my father insisted on acknowledging me as his daughter on my birth certificate, so I have dual nationality and two passports. I'm Calanthe Reynolds, as you knew me, and Calanthe Petranakos as well.'

He saw her expression change. Harden with suspicion.

'How did you know I was taking the ferry?' she asked.

He smiled, eyes glinting. 'Your housekeeper told me when I phoned this morning to offer to escort you to the party,' he said.

Calanthe's eyes flashed angrily. 'I neither need nor want your escort!' Her face worked. 'Leave me *alone*, Nik. I don't want *anything* to do with you ever again! I made that clear enough at Sounion. Our "summer romance", as you call it, was over eight years ago. You saw to that.' The bitterness in her voice was audible, and something hardened in her eyes. 'You're not getting another one.'

He met her flashing eyes full-on. This time

neither of them was wearing shades, and he could see the angry depths of her grey-blue eyes…eyes that had once gazed at him meltingly, filled with warmth and desire and passion and something more than that…

'Maybe,' he said slowly, his eyes never leaving hers, 'a summer romance is no longer what I want. Maybe I've moved on, Calanthe. Maybe I want something more.'

It was strange to say it. Strange to put it into words. But as he did so, he knew he meant it. Although just what 'more' was it that he wanted?

That he did not know. Not yet…

But his words had drawn a reaction from her—an instant withdrawal. He heard her sharp intake of breath. Then he saw her shoulders hunch as she flicked open the journal she was clutching.

She didn't look up as she threw her reply at him. 'Too bad, Nik. Because you will never do to me again what you did before. *Never.*'

There was anger in her voice. And more than anger. A bleakness that was like a knife twisting in his guts. He frowned inwardly, suddenly on edge. He masked his expression, relieved she wasn't looking at him. Felt the twist in his guts come again. Urgently he tried to untwist it. To reassure himself.

She can't know—I made it clear that she must never know. Never.

She must never know what he had done that summer long ago...

Calanthe heard the bleakness in her own voice and knew why it was there. The words on the page of her journal blurred, then resolved into focus again. A focus she must keep now, doggedly, despite the turmoil in her brain.

Her nerves were totally overset. She had accepted Marina's invitation as an opportunity to get her away from Athens, away from Nikos—and now here he was, sitting right opposite her, heading to the very destination she was. She could not bear it.

Determinedly, she buried herself in her journal, totally ignoring the man sitting opposite her. Yet she was aware that he had got his phone out, was perusing the screen, occupying himself as she was.

After a while, he got to his feet. 'I think I'll stretch my legs,' he remarked.

Calanthe made no reply, conscious that she could now minutely relax. To her relief he didn't come back—not even when the ferry finally docked.

She hung back deliberately, hoping he'd take a taxi up to the Volous villa, but when she did disembark—for the ferry was about to set off to the next island on its itinerary—to her dismay there he was, down on the dock, leaning casually against the door of a svelte saloon car that had drawn up on the cobbles.

He waved as she walked off the ferry, carrying her overnight bag with her. 'Our hosts have sent a car to collect us,' he said, opening the rear passenger door and relieving her of her bag, though she had not asked him to.

Stiffly, she got in, murmuring something to the driver, and was grateful that Nikos got into the front passenger seat. The car set off, nosing down the narrow streets to gain the open road and then head along the coast road towards the Volous villa.

Calanthe had been there once before, the previous year, when her friend Marina had first married, and she knew it to be large and luxurious, set above its own private beach, with a multitude of guest rooms. She would ensure hers was far away from Nikos.

Her face set stonily. Nikos was chatting to the driver in an easy-going fashion and memory assailed her. Nik had always chatted easily to anyone—he'd fitted in with the student crowd that summer, been accepted by them as one of their own, and now he was chatting easily to a man who earned his living working as a driver for a very wealthy couple.

But then, that is Nik's own background, isn't it? Nothing grand or privileged...

Unease flickered through her. On the ferry she'd thrown at him the way she'd been raised by her mother. Yet he had thought her to be faking it—faking the person she'd presented herself as during that summer.

Should I have told him who I was?

Her expression hardened. It would have made no difference, though, would it? Not in the end...

The car drove through electronically controlled gates, crunched along a driveway and pulled up. The driver came round to open Calanthe's door. She got out, murmuring her thanks, feeling the heat hit her after the air-conditioning of the car. The driver was getting her bag, hefting out another one too—Nikos's, she assumed—and then taking the car away to wherever the garages were. The front door of the grand villa was opening, and a member of staff was welcoming them in.

Saying not a word to Nikos, Calanthe hurried forward, eager to gain the sanctuary of her own room. Eager, above all, to be nowhere near the man she wanted absolutely nothing to do with.

Calanthe! Darling! *Wonderful* to see you here!'

Marina, who had always been the exuberant

type, sailed forward, her red and gold kaftan billowing in the breeze that lifted up from the beach to reach the wide marbled pool terrace already thronged with arriving guests gathering for afternoon cocktails.

Calanthe, having finally reluctantly emerged from her room, knowing she could not hide there for ever, was gushingly embraced, and then Marina stood back, her dark eyes gleaming with blatant curiosity.

'So, darling, tell me *all* about that absolutely *gorgeous* hunk of a man you've brought with you! Theo tells me he invited him—but it's you he arrived with! So, tell *all*!'

Calanthe stepped back from Marina's embrace, feigning indifference. 'We just came in the same car, that's all. He's a business acquaintance of my father—that's how I know him.'

Marina's gleam intensified. 'Playing it cool, are you? Well, no change there, then! Except...' her voice became conspiratorial '...the absolutely *gorgeous* Nikos Kavadis is in a league of his own compared with all your usual boyfriends!'

'He is *not* my boyfriend!' The words snapped from Calanthe. 'I told you—I hardly know him.'

'Hardly know him *yet*,' Marina amended. 'And tonight will be the *perfect* time to remedy that. Mind you,' she added, 'you'll have to move

fast. He's already being sized up by every preda-
tory female here!'

'They are totally welcome to him,' Calanthe
informed her. 'Marina, please… Don't try and…
well, you know.'

Her friend threw her hands up. 'You'll fall one
day, darling! Even you! Little Miss Cool will
melt eventually… I warn you!'

Calanthe remained expressionless, but emotion knifed inside her. Marina's warning was far
too late. Eight years too late.

Involuntarily, her eyes went to the far side of
the swimming pool. Nikos was there, talking
to Marina's husband and several other people.
Talking as easily as he'd talked to the driver on
the way up here. Quite at home in these wealthy
surroundings. Just as he'd been quite at home in
Athens' most expensive hotel, where her father
had held his birthday celebration.

And he was looking as devastating as he always did.

Always had.

Whether he was in his rough work clothes on
the construction site or, as now, in the kind of
eye-wateringly expensive designer label casual
clothes suitable for a high society villa party in
the Aegean. And Marina was right—many female eyes were going his way. Eyeing him up.
Wondering if he was available…

A sour expression crossed Calanthe's face.

Help yourself, ladies! You'll be doing me *a* *favour.*

Marina was asking her what she'd like t drink, and beckoning a circling member of he staff.

Calanthe shook her head. 'Actually, what I' really like to do is catch a swim,' she said.

'Darling, of course! There's the pool!' Marin gestured expansively.

'Oh, no—I was thinking of the beach. The se looks so inviting. I'll just run down...'

She slipped away. Under the sundress she' changed into in her room she'd put on a one piece swimsuit. Towels would be supplied at th beach, she knew. She could hide there until was time to come in and dress for the evening

The path down to the beach zigzagge through the garden, opening up eventually ont clear pebbled sand. Sun loungers had been so out under parasols, each with a bale of towel. There was a little changing room as well, to on side, as well as a small and pretty blue-shuttere beach house, set back from the beach.

But all Calanthe had to do was pull off he sundress, and head for the water. It was cool an refreshing and she gave a sigh of relief as it em braced her. Slowly, she swam out to sea, wantin to calm her ragged nerves. She was stuck here ti tomorrow morning at the earliest. If she cut and ran now Marina would want to know why, and that would cause yet more of the speculation that was the last thing Calanthe wanted to encourage.

Please, please, let Nik pair off with someone else! Let him accept I won't have anything to do with him again and find consolation elsewhere.

There would certainly be women ready to offer that consolation. And Nik could pull any of them.

He always could. Even when he was just a penniless student. No woman could resist him... Least of all me...

She turned on her back, letting her hair float out around her, and lifted her face to the westering sun, feeling its rays warming her cheeks even though the water was keeping the rest of her cool. As she drifted, arms splayed out for buoyancy, eyes closed against the bright sun, cradled by the warm Aegean sea, a memory seeped into her synapses.

A memory she could not hold at bay.

A memory she could not resist...

Even as she had not been able to resist Nik.

Their first night of passion...incandescent... unforgettable...

He'd been wooing her for a week. Seducing her slowly but surely. She knew it—welcomed it. Gloried in it. And now, this Friday night, she pulled out all the stops for him.

She and Georgia had been shopping, each determined to dress up for the evening, giggling as they made their choices.

Georgia wore a mini-dress, showing off her long legs, but Calanthe had opted for a vermilion floaty, calf-length peasant-style gathered skirt and an embroidered blouson, worn off her shoulders, and espadrilles to make her taller. She was letting her glorious hair cascade freely down her back. And when she saw the look in Nik's eyes as she approached she knew with every female instinct that tonight...oh, tonight... the kisses she had come to yearn for would become so much more...

When the lively meal finally ended, and only the hardcore students remained, she and Nikos stood up from the table. Georgia and Dave were leaning close, heads together, murmuring sweet nothings to each other, and she was glad for them.

Gladder still for herself.

Was she in love? She didn't know. She only knew the wonder that netted her and the way her heart lifted every time she saw Nik. The way her pulse quickened, her breathing became shallow, and the way she longed for him to sweep her up to him, wind his strong arms around her, bend his mouth to hers...

And she knew that he, and he alone, was all that she wanted and craved...

They wandered through the warm Aegean night, his arm around her waist, she leaning into him, down the cobbled streets to where his little pensione was. He was taking her to his place, for she knew that Georgia would want the room they shared in their own little apartment for herself and Dave.

And she was ready for this—totally, completely ready.

He kissed her in the doorway, slow and sensuous, arousing, then asked, 'Is this what you want? You must be sure, Calanthe.'

His dark eyes poured into hers.

She wound her arms around his neck.

'Yes,' she breathed. 'Oh...yes!'

He smiled and led her indoors, up the narrow wooden stairs. Inside his room it was warm, but a thread of cooling breeze came through the open window overlooking the harbour. The narrow bed awaited them—with just room for two.

He turned her to him, smiled down at her. 'This week,' he said huskily, 'has been an eternity.'

Then slowly, very slowly, he eased down the loosely gathered neckline of her blouson, slipping it over her shoulders...exposing her breasts...lowering his mouth to graze their ripening mounds.

She gave a moan of pleasure, leaning back, and felt her nipples cresting. Each gliding soft caress of his mouth, of the tingling tip of his tongue as it laved her, sent ripples of exquisite bliss through her.

Her moan came again, and then, as he lifted his mouth away from her, it became a cry of loss.

He smiled. 'Oh, sweet Calanthe, the feast has only just begun...'

And he showed her.

He slid the blouson from her...slid down, too, the gathered skirt, so that it fell in a dark pool to the floor. She stood there with only her wispy panties remaining. He reached out a finger to her, never taking his eyes from hers, and ran it along the waistline of the material. She thought she must die of bliss.

But the bliss, like the feast, had only just begun.

He eased the material down and she stepped out of it. Her heart was beating like a drum, her pulse throbbing in her veins. She heard his breath catch.

'So beautiful...' There was a husk in his voice...a rasp.

She smiled. 'Your turn,' she said.

She reached for him, slid open each button of his shirt one by one, achingly and arousingly slowly, easing the shirt away to let her finger-

...ps explore beneath. He stood stock-still, and
...ith an instinct as old as Eve, she knew he was
...xerting every inch of his self-control to stand
...ere while she slid the shirt from him.

Then she turned her hands to the belt around
...s waist. As she undid the buckle, feeling her
...ay in the dim light, she gave a sudden gasp of
...ock. Her hands had felt, unmistakably, just
...w much self-control he was exerting.

A low laugh broke from him, but there was ur-
...ncy in his voice when he spoke. 'This is a tor-
...ent such as I do not think I can endure,' he said.

He lifted her hands away with his own strong
...nds, callused and rough from his work on the
...ilding site. Swiftly, he finished what she had
...arted, and as he shucked himself free of his
...ousers and his shorts she gave another gasp.
...stinctively turned away.

He caught her in his arms, scooped her up
...fortlessly against his muscled frame, then
...ossed over to the bed, pulled back the cover-
...g sheet and laid her down as gently as if she
...ere made of porcelain.

Then he lowered himself beside her. 'Shall we
...gin?' he asked.

His voice was low and accented, filled with
...hat she knew with all her being to be desire.

His hand glided along her flank, shaping her
...east, leisurely exploring it, then moved over

the soft, slender mound of her belly to slip his questing fingers over her thighs, between them...

They slackened at his touch and she gave another low, instinctive moan. What he was doing to her was exquisite—unbearable...

Sensation such as she had not known existed, had not known possible, teased through her, and she felt her hands clench into the bedding. She felt arousal sweeten inside her and knew that he was readying her body for his possession.

He moved his strong, hard thighs over hers, widened her legs...

'Nik—I... I've never...'

The words broke from her and he stilled. Gazed down at her. For a few seconds he did not speak, and for a dreadful moment, she thought he would draw back.

Then he lowered his mouth to hers. 'You give me a gift,' he said, 'that any man would treasure.' He grazed her mouth again, the smile at his lips rueful. 'I will be as gentle as I can,' he told her.

He was true to his promise. There was pain, as she knew there must be, but it lasted such a little time compared with the eternity of bliss he gave her...

Again and again, and yet again, she felt her spine arch in ecstasy as he held her trembling body in his arms. Her own arms wound around him tightly, as if she would never, never let him

go. It was bliss, it was wonder, and it was be-
yond all she had imagined such a time would be.

And then finally, as her own bliss ebbed and
she felt the low throb of her own body enclosing
his, drawing him in deeper, and deeper yet, he
lifted his body from her and drove, with strong,
powerful thrusts, to bring his own release.

As he did so, her body convulsed around his
yet again...more intensely, more searingly. She
cried out—she could not help it—her hands
clutching at him, feeling the strain of his mus-
cles, seeing his throat tensing as his body expe-
rienced what she was experiencing yet again. A
groan broke from him, low and harsh, and his
forehead lowered to hers as if in salutation.

She took him into her embrace, feeling a won-
der and a joy and a happiness so great she could
not measure it. He folded into her and she cra-
dled him, feeling the sweet weight of his body on
hers, smoothing his dampened hair, his muscled
shoulders, soothing him, caressing him, cher-
ishing him...

Loving him...

Was it tears in her eyes now, or simply the sea
water wetting her cheeks? Well, what did it matter? The Nik she had known then—or thought
she had known—was gone with the years.

She would not let him back in.

Dared not.

Whatever the temptation.

The word was in her head before she coul
stop it. Shocking her. Dismaying her.

With a gasp, she jack-knifed in the water, he
wet hair clinging to her shoulders, and trod wate
rapidly. No, no—of *course* she wasn't bein
tempted by him! How could she even think it'

For a moment she threshed in the water, push
ing her soggy hair out of her eyes, and then, wit
an effort, duck dived into the clear sea. She ha
drifted quite far out. There were rocks below, o
the seabed, small fishes darting, and she coul
feel the swell of open water.

Arcing around, she surfaced, looking back t
shore. Only to see, with deeper dismay, as sh
blinked the water from her lashes, the tall figur
of Nikos standing by the shoreline.

He was looking directly at her.

Nikos put his hands around his mouth to am
plify his voice. 'You're very far out! Need a tov
back in?'

He lowered his hands as he saw her strike ou
towards the shore in a strong freestyle. He'd won
dered whether to go in and fetch her, but she wa
doing OK. He watched until she was back withi
her depth. She was clearly reluctant to get out c
the water with him watching. Should he do th

gentlemanly thing and turn his back? Let her reach her lounger and wrap a towel around her?

No. He would not. But what he did do was fetch the towel for her, shake it open.

'Think of me as a beach valet,' he informed her drily.

Expressionlessly, she waded out. Not looking at him.

It was something he found he could not reciprocate. Instead, he fastened his gaze on her, in her clinging one-piece.

Her coltish figure had matured into a softer, richer form, yet her legs were still as toned, her body still as slender. The simple swimsuit moulded her body to perfection, and the cold of the water had done delectable things to her nipples...

He felt a kick in his pulse that he could not stop...felt arousal stir and knew he must turn away, just as she was doing, having snatched the towel from him.

Rigorously she wrapped it around herself, busying herself with squeezing out her dripping hair. 'I don't appreciate you following me down here!' she snapped.

He was back in control of himself.

'I did not follow you,' he informed her. 'As a late invite, I've been put in the beach house.' He gestured to the small stone-built building set back from the beach, its whitewashed walls and blue shutters and door lit by the rich late-afternoon sunshine. 'Simple accommodation, no staff service, but ideal for midnight swims,' he said good-humouredly. His eyes glinted. 'Perhaps you'll join me for one tonight?'

She glowered fiercely at him, but he was not put off.

'Lighten up, Calanthe—this is a weekend to enjoy.' He made his voice still humorous, but there was a message in it all the same.

She was yanking at her hair, starting to rapidly and roughly plait it.

'So enjoy it!' she told him. 'Just not with me! There are any number of women all too willing to help you do so, I'm sure!'

His eyes rested on her face. 'The thing is, Calanthe, the only one I want is you...'

He had softened his voice. Made it a caress.

An invitation.

A promise.

He felt emotions move within him. Desire, yes—for who could not feel desire as she stood there? Even with the beach towel obliterating her figure and her fingers working on her dripping hair, her face shining with sea water and bereft of any make-up. His breath caught. Whatever it was about her, he could not take his eyes from her. Could not stop these strange emotions welling up within him.

This time… This time we'll make it come right between us.

That was the promise in his head.

To himself.

To her.

She'd stilled, her fingers still entwined in her half-plaited her. He changed his expression. Became reminiscent, softened his tone more.

'You used to plait your hair like that in the morning when we were getting up together. You were heading back to the dig and I was putting in my shift at the construction site. You'd pin it up, and I'd have to wait all day until finally I could take those damn pins out, unplait it, and let it tumble around your shoulders. We'd fall into bed, then shower, then get dressed and go and join the others at the taverna. You would look… oh, so lovely. Your eyes glowing from our lovemaking…your skin honey from the sun… And we'd sit together at the table, and you'd sneak some of my deep-fried aubergines, which you never ordered for yourself because you said they were too fattening. But somehow nicking mine wasn't fattening at all…'

He gave a low laugh, memory vivid in his head.

'Don't—' Her voice was low. Strained. 'There's no point remembering, Nik. It was eight years ago. It's not coming back.'

He shook his head. 'No, it's not coming back. But…' He changed his voice again and felt his arm lifting of its own volition, as if to reach for her. 'But we can—'

'Can what?' She cut across him, and her voice was like a blade. 'Pick up where we left off? Is that your idea? You bump into me, eight years on, and think, *Hey, she's still fanciable…why don't I take another tour?*'

She was standing so close he'd only have to take a step towards her to reach for her, but her stance was rigid…chin lifted, eyes stony.

'It's not like that,' he said tightly. 'Look…' he frowned '…eight years ago I had nothing—nothing except responsibilities. Responsibilities to complete my training, make something of myself any way I could…'

He saw something changing in her face, but he ignored it. This was important—he had to make her understand. Understand that now was not then.

'And now I have! I'm a wealthy man. And, whilst I still have a great deal I want to do with my life, things that I want to achieve—as you do, I'm sure, in your own field—I've got time now. Real time to want more than I wanted eight years ago. And what I want…*who* I want…' his voice softened again as his eyes rested on her unflinchingly, openly '…is you.' He took a breath.

I told you that at Sounion. Told you that even if I'd never known you before I would want you now. And, no—not just for a summer romance! Calanthe, this…between us…could be something else. Something that might prove really important…in my life.' He paused. 'You're important to me, Calanthe—I want you to know that.'

She didn't answer. Her hands had fallen to her sides as he'd spoken to her, saying the things he knew he had to say. He could not read her face, though he searched her eyes. Then she took a breath.

'I'm going up to shower and change,' she said.

She walked to where her sundress was lying on the lounger, picked it up. Turned back to him as she slipped her feet into flat sandals. Took another breath and looked straight at him. Face expressionless.

'Stay away from me tonight,' she told him.

Then she turned and headed for the path, making her way up through the gardens.

Nikos watched her till she was lost to sight.

Stay away from me tonight.

Her words echoed in his head, and his own answer echoed too.

I can't.

CHAPTER SIX

CALANTHE GAVE HER appearance once last check, relieved that she had brought this particular dress to wear this evening. It was Grecian-style, a pale column of finely pleated ivory silk, the bodice draping over her torso, and it made her look cool and elegant.

Statuesque.

Not in the least enticing.

That was the last thing she wanted.

But once…

Memory flickered like a flame she wanted to quench, yet still flickered for all that.

That vivid vermilion peasant skirt…the off-the-shoulder embroidered blouson…her hair loose and tumbling…

All to lure Nik.

There was a sour taste in her mouth. Oh, Nik had got lucky that summer, all right! She'd fallen for him totally, given herself to him totally, wanting nothing more in all the world than him! And he… Well, he'd helped himself to her—to more than what she'd offered him so very gladly…

She pulled her mind away, out of the past. She could not bear to think about it now.

Back in the present, his words on the beach hung in the space between herself and her reflection.

'You're important to me, Calanthe.'

Her expression steeled. Yet in the pit of her stomach she could feel what she'd never wanted to feel ever again. The wash of hot, humid humiliation that she could not bear to acknowledge, to face, or to admit. She turned away, not wanting to see the woman in the mirror…the woman who could be 'important' to Nikos Kavadis.

She would not be that woman.

Reluctantly, she crossed to the bedroom door. She had taken refuge in her room, performing lengthy ablutions, taking for ever over her hair, even though it was simply coiled in a soft chignon at her nape, and a long time over her make-up, even though it was the bare minimum for such an evening.

She had taken as long as she could, even asking one of the maids to bring her some Earl Grey tea as she dressed for the evening, but she could delay no longer—or Marina would send out a search party. Already she could hear music coming in through the glass doors to her balcony.

Nerving herself, she went to join the party.

Nikos stood at the far end of the terrace, looking out over the darkened sea beyond. His mood was strange. He had accepted the invitation to this party for one reason only—because he knew, from Georgios Petranakos, that Calanthe had been invited too.

Georgios was being assiduous in letting him know his daughter's social diary. Nikos's eyes narrowed. He knew there was a reason for Georgios's co-operation in his pursuit of Calanthe. Georgios hadn't spelt it out—he hadn't needed to—but Nikos had got the message. It was common knowledge that without a son—and given that Calanthe had no interest in her father's business herself—Georgios Petranakos would be on the lookout for a son-in-law of sufficient calibre to take over the running of his property empire when his time was up.

And I may just make the grade.

There was an irony to that which was not lost on him. Eight years had changed his prospects radically. If Georgios Petranakos really was assessing him in the way he might be, it should reassure him—show him that this time his interest in Georgios's daughter would not be opposed

Not if he carried it through to the conclusion that Georgios might just have in mind.

But do I have it in mind? Is it something I would consider?

He felt his thoughts move over the question. He had told Calanthe down on the beach now veiled in the darkness of the evening that she was important to him. But what had he meant by that? He did not know—not yet.

I need to make her mine again—need to claim her back. I need to hold her in my arms...to know...discover again...what she is to me.

He shifted restlessly, feeling his thoughts just as restless. Sightlessly, he gazed out over the darkened sea stretching to the horizon. There were no lights to steer by, only the stars above, and someone would have to know the constellations to navigate by them.

For him, it was his own future he was trying to reach—would it be Calanthe's too?

His unease sharpened. What if the past had already blighted the future?

His hands tightened over the stone balustrade and he lifted his head. Determination fired in his eyes. He must steer his course by his own judgement. He had always done so and would not change now.

Taking a breath, he lifted his hands away

and headed back along the terrace to where the bright lights of the party were beckoning him.

And where Calanthe awaited him.

Calanthe was surrounding herself with people all dressed up for the evening, the men in white dinner jackets, the women in silky evening gowns. Most of those she was with she already knew, so after greetings had been exchanged it meant she could get away with contributing little to the general conversation. She was sipping at champagne, but making a glass last a long time, then swapping it for sparkling mineral water.

Always she knew where Nikos was.

Right now he was on the far side of the pool, in another circle of people. To her relief he had made no attempt to talk to her, or even approach her. Nor did he move in on the people she was with. To her even greater relief he was clearly being targeted by a very determined woman, bejewelled to the nines, with bleached blonde hair, too much make-up, and a very clinging short dress.

Nikos was welcome to her.

Please let him content himself with whoever that is throwing herself at him! Please let me just get through enough of the evening to be able to retire without Marina coming to drag me out again! And please don't let her think there is anything at all between me and Nikos Kavadis!

To aid herself in this plea Calanthe knew that she, too, must display some diversionary tactics. Provide a decoy. Yannis, as it happened, was not here—he was away in New York on business—but an even better decoy was on hand. Bastian.

Bastian was ideal. He was a long-time admirer but, since he was also one of Athens' most assiduous playboys, his pursuit of her would be for one purpose only—another notch on his very well-notched bedpost. But he was also good-humoured and easy-going, and she knew all she had to do was let him know she was trying to avoid a particular man here and he would co-operate happily.

An hour later he was doing just that.

A lavish buffet was being served, and everyone was taking their places at the tables set out under colourful lights strung overhead.

A covert glance from Calanthe showed her that Nikos and the bleached blonde were at a table as far away from where she was as it was possible to be. Sitting herself down beside Bastian, finding their own table lively in the extreme, she finally started to relax. Helped, she knew, by the second glass of champagne Bastian had presented her with.

'Drink up, my sweet,' he murmured shamelessly in her ear. 'Then I might finally stand a chance with you this evening…'

She pushed him away good-humouredly and took another sip of her champagne, feeling the net of unbearable tension easing from her. She would get through supper, dance a couple of times with Bastian, and then escape. Plead a headache…whatever… It didn't matter. And tomorrow she would head back to Athens.

All she had to do was get through the rest of the evening.

As for Nikos—

She cut off her thoughts. Banned them from her head. She laughed, instead, at something one of her friends at the table had just said, taking more sips of champagne in between mouthfuls of the delicious gourmet buffet Marina's chef had provided.

I can do this. I can do it because I must. Just as, when I'm back in Athens, I can keep doing it. If Nikos tries to contact me again I will simply stonewall him. I will have nothing more to do with him. Nothing. Not tonight…not in Athens. Not ever.

Yet even as she made the vow to herself she felt her eyes slipping sideways as she reached again for her champagne glass…slipping across the array of candlelit tables to the one where Nikos was seated.

She didn't want to look, yet some kind of com-
ulsion made her do it all the same, and he was
tting so that she could see his profile…see him
an a little towards the woman at his side…see
im smile at her.

A needle slid into her heart. Once it had been
er he'd smiled at and her alone. A private smile,
arm and intimate, full of promise and fulfilment.

She felt an ache arise inside her, a longing…

Her fingers convulsed over the slender stem
f her champagne flute. Dear God, she must not
llow such memories! So painful, so aching…
o dangerous.

She felt a hand touch her bare forearm and
arted.

'If I were the jealous type…' Bastian trailed
ff, an eyebrow lifting, his eyes slanting to
here she had been looking.

She gave a sharp shake of her head. Dismiss-
g the insinuation. She took another mouthful
f champagne and set down the glass, resum-
g her meal. Doggedly, for the rest of supper,
e refused to let her eyes go anywhere near the
ne man in all the world she must not look at.

Must not have anything to do with ever again.

Must not crave…

ikos smiled at the woman beside him. He
ished her no ill, but she was wasting her time.

She'd already told him she was newly divorced, her unfaithful ex-husband set aside, and that all she wanted right now was to feel good about herself again in the aftermath by reminding herself that she could still draw male attention.

Well, he had a solution to her predicament— but it was not going to be himself.

His eyes narrowed. Watching—or rather *not* watching Calanthe devote herself to a man who all of Athens knew to be a notorious playboy was not an enjoyable process. His only comfort was that he knew why she was doing it. And he knew what he was going to do about it.

But he must pick his time carefully. Get it just right. And then—

He cut his thoughts off. He must not rush ahead of himself—must not make assumptions or take it for granted that he would achieve what he was set upon.

A wry expression formed in his eyes. Eight years ago he had known that Calanthe's initial prickly attitude to him had been a disguise for her response to him. Known that once he got past that—as he had so very easily in the end— she would yield to her response to him…yield to his desire for her. The desire with which he'd kindled hers, set it aflame…

But she was fighting him now every centimetre of the way—he could take nothing for granted.

I only know that she is fighting not just me, but herself as well...

Well, he would not give up on her.

Not this time.

This time he would make it all come right between them.

Calanthe was dancing with Bastian. She'd lingered at the supper table, not wanting to exert herself in the upbeat dance numbers that the live band had struck up with, waiting for something slower. Now she was wishing she hadn't. She'd made it clear to Bastian that she only wanted him as a decoy, nothing else, but he'd been knocking back the champagne, and now he was making every effort to get up close and personal with her, however often she drew herself away from him.

The moment the number ended she'd make her excuses and leave.

She didn't get the chance.

'Time to trade partners,' said a cool, deep voice behind her.

She froze, but it was too late. Nikos had simply disengaged Bastian's hands from around her waist and blatantly put them around the waist of his own partner—the bleached blonde, Calanthe

saw instantly. She also saw that both the blond
and Bastian were taken aback, but then, as the
eyed each other up, were swiftly reconciled t
the exchange. She heard Bastian pay his new
partner an extravagant compliment, saw her tos
her head and smile encouragingly, and then the
were away.

As for herself…

'Finally,' said Nikos, in the same cool, dee
voice.

And took her into his arms.

She was as rigid as the marble statute she re
sembled. Yet the hands that had come to res
automatically on his shoulders were trem
bling—he could feel it through the linen c
his white tuxedo jacket. Just as he could fee
the warmth of her body through the delicat
plissé material of her dress as his hands reste
at her waist.

Sensation washed through him.

To hold her again…have her in his arms…

With an effort that cost him more than h
wanted to exert, he kept his touch as light as h
could, resisting the overpowering temptation t
draw her to him, feel the soft length of her bod
moulded against his.

She was far, far too tense for that.

And she was pulling away from him. Oh, n

obviously, but her spine was arching back, her feet moving back the maximum distance they could, given he was holding her and dancing.

For a second she looked at him, her eyes wide with shock. Then she yanked her gaze past him.

'Let me go,' she said.

Her voice was as tight as the drawstring of a bow.

'Dance with me,' he said.

His voice was low in pitch, for her ears alone.

He felt her straining back and thought she would pull free of him—which she could easily do, for his hands were barely touching her waist. Yet she did not.

'I won't make a scene,' she said, her voice still bowstring-tight, still looking straight past him. 'That's the only reason.'

'That's good enough for me,' Nikos murmured, his voice relaxing, his stance relaxing.

Carefully, he started to move, picking up on the slow, familiar melody from the band as the singer started to croon the lyrics of an old sentimental song.

They danced, but hardly moved. To his side, almost out of his sightline, Nikos could see the divorced blonde draping herself over a very willing Bastian, whose hands were now freely running up and down her back. He wished them well. Wished everyone in the entire world well.

For one reason only.

Calanthe was in his arms.

The only place he wanted her to be.

How she got through the dance she didn't know. It seemed to go on for an eternity. Or perhaps eternity was being in Nikos's arms...

Yet he was barely touching her, his hands hardly skimming the fabric of her gown, and her own hands were barely skimming the fabric of his jacket. Nor was she looking at him. She could not. Dared not.

Yet her consciousness of what she was doing—what he was doing—was like an enveloping flame...a flame that licked at her senses, flickered along her nerves, grazed her bare skin.

A line from the Ancient Greek, old and familiar, came to her:

...subtle fire runs like a thief through my body...

The poetess Sappho, whose lost verses remained only in shattered fragments.

As my love for Nikos was shattered.

But she could not think of that—could not feel that now. Could only feel what it was to be here, in his arms, in an embrace that was barely there. Yet she could catch the scent of his aftershave, the scent of his body, and knew that all she had to do was step closer to him, fold her hands over his strong shoulders, let his hands fasten around her pliant waist, bend her to him, turn her head so that his mouth could catch at hers…

Fire and faintness…faintness and fire…yearning and wanting…wanting and yearning.

There was nothing else…nothing in all the world, all the universe. Only this slow eternal dance.

And then it ended. The music stopped. Though the pulse in her veins did not. Nor did the fire still running through her body like the thief it was…

She felt his hands drop from her…let her own hands fall…let her eyes finally meet his.

And in them she saw what she must not accept, must not acknowledge. Must not permit.

Instinctively she moved away. She saw the dark outline of the path that led off the terrace, away from the light, away from the party…away from Nikos. It offered refuge from him, from the pulse of her own veins, the fire stealing her senses and her sense.

The sound of the cicadas in the lush, irrigated vegetation was loud in her ears as the noise of the party dimmed. All around, the heady scent of jasmine infused her senses. A little way along, the path widened into a miniature terrace, only a few metres square, with a stone bench at one side. She sank down on it, looking out towards the night-black sea, still feeling that heady pulse in her veins, the flicker of fire that she could not put out.

Footsteps on the path leading to the little terrace stayed her. A figure emerged. Tall and dark. Only the white of his jacket visible in the starlight. Her breath caught.

'Calanthe…' said Nikos.

His voice was as velvet as the night.

She did not move, and yet he heard the low intake of her breath, saw her eyes going to his in the dim light spilling through the leaves from the party above.

He walked towards her, his pace unhurried.

She got to her feet, stood there as if poised for flight. But she made no move.

Her eyes had flared wide…her lips had parted. She stood stock-still, as still as a marble column, in her ivory silk gown, her arms slender, her throat exposed, hair in tendrils around her face.

He lifted a hand to her, his fingers drifting with infinite slowness down the smooth length of her bare arm, and took her nerveless hand in his. He felt her tremble at his touch. His gaze burned into her widened eyes. Her lips were still parted. Motionless. And she was so exquisitely beautiful that his muscles clenched, holding his body taut.

Slowly, infinitely slowly, he drew drifting fingers down her other arm, took her other hand in his, hearing another intake of her breath. Her hands were warm and trembling in his clasp.

'Nikos…'

It was a breath of air, no more than that. A whisper. A plea.

'Don't—please…*please* don't…'

He gazed down at her.

'Don't what, Calanthe?'

His voice was husky now, his whole body held under such control that it racked him.

'Don't tell you how beautiful you are? How I desire you?' That half-smile, mocking himself, twisted at his mouth again. 'I wanted you then, all those years ago—and I want you now.'

He felt his want rise within him, flushing his veins like a slow, ineluctable tide, infusing his senses. The scent of jasmine was drowning the perfumed air. From above, the low throb of music pulsed.

He saw her eyes dip closed, then open again, with a new pleading in them.

'Nikos—I can't. I won't—' She broke off and half turned away, drawing one hand away from his.

With his freed hand he cupped her averted cheek, felt her skin like satin.

'Don't turn away.' The huskiness was stronger now, the self-control more urgent. 'Don't turn away from this. From what this is. From what has always been between us. From the very first…'

Slowly, carefully, he turned her to look at him again. Her eyes were flared so wide he could see into their depths. See, with a stab of triumph, the distension of her pupils.

Her words might deny him.

Her body could not…

He said her name again, husky and lingering. Bent his mouth to hers. Felt the tender softness of her lips. She made no resistance and triumph came again. But it dissolved even as it came, liquefying into desire, drumming at his senses, flooding his blood, his brain, with its power and potency.

All evening he'd seen her, so near and yet so far. He'd known he would close in on her. Known that was the reason he was here at all. Known it was his purpose. His intent.

And now…*now* it was happening. He was claiming her back…

Had he been a fool, eight years ago, to part with her as he had? Whatever the reason he had done so? He didn't know—could not answer… could not care. His senses were reeling, the exertion of holding his body in check bringing agony to his muscles.

He heard through the drumming of his pulse her breathing his name again. But nothing else. No protest. No denial.

Only yielding... To my desire. To her own desire.

His kiss deepened on her tremulous lips, opening her mouth, oh, so softly to his.

He felt his body surge. His hand tightened on hers as he drew his mouth away. He lifted his fingers to her still-parted lips, tracing their outline. Slowly, lingeringly. She gazed up at him, making no move away from him.

He smiled. A smile for her and her alone in this moment which had come at last.

'Come,' he said.

He led her on down the sloping path to the beach below. Dimly she was aware of the soft sound of wavelets breaking gently on the pebbled shore, of the starlight high above them, the cradling darkness of the night. She could not speak, could not think...could do nothing but let him lead her.

Why she was doing this she did not know. It made no sense. It was everything she had said she must not yield to. And yet she was yielding.

Fragments of thought fleeted through her mind as he led her onwards.

This time he cannot hurt me—because this time I know him for what he is...know the hurt

*he did me. So if I yield to him—yield to all that .
can deny no longer, all that I crave for myself—
then surely it will be for me alone, with no illusions. Only desire.*

Desire she could no longer deny, or resist, o
in any way do anything but yield to now, in this
moment, in this night…

Her hand in his, they reached the little ston
beach house and he pushed open the door. Drev
her inside. Into his arms.

They lit no lamps. Needed no light. Only the
dim reflection from the phosphorescence off the
sea through the single window beside the wide
bed. Her ivory gown was skimmed from he
trembling body, his own impeding clothes ruth
lessly, impatiently discarded, and he drew he
down, laying her softly on the white sheet, low
ering his lean, hard body beside her.

Covering her body with his.

As he had done before, so long ago.

And now he did it again.

She was silk and satin, her body slender stil
but softer in the fullness of her womanhood. Sh
was everything he remembered and so muc
more.

With slow sensuality he explored every part c
her, drowning in his own pleasure as he did s
drawing from her a pleasure that showed in he

eyes fluttering shut, in the low, helpless moans from her throat.

He moved over her, cupping her breasts, feeling them engorge at his touch, her nipples cresting between his gently scissoring fingers. Her eyes flew open, then fluttered shut again, and he saw pleasure flush her face, arch her neck. He lowered his mouth to her breast, suckling at her with slow swirls of his tongue, lingering and leisurely, then administered the same to her other breast.

He reared back to gaze at her. A smile curved his lips as he looked down at her lying there, splayed on his bed, head back, breasts ripened by his touch, hands outstretched, fingers curved into the sheet. A low, husky laugh of triumph and desire, arousal and possession came from him, and then he was lowering himself to her again, easing his body so that his hands could cup her hips, letting his lips glide over the soft curve of her waistline and further still.

He slipped one hand from her hip, parting her thighs, cupping the secret V between with the heel of his hand. He heard her moan again, felt her hands folding over his shoulders, her nails indenting into his muscled flesh. He moulded her with the heel of his hand, feeling her body's response.

Then he lifted his hand away.

Lowered his mouth instead.

His conscious mind was in white-out. There was nothing in the universe except this and now. Heat was burning up his own body as his tongue and lips feasted where, when he had readied her, he would possess her fully. Her moans were coming faster now, more helpless. He heard her head thrashing on the pillow, felt her thighs widen and slacken, her hips lifting in automatic, instinctive and overpowering pleading. He heard her say his name. Low and incoherent. Arousal was coursing through him, so powerful it was impossible to restrain himself any longer, not for a moment, not an instant...

He lifted his head away and reared over her, his hands sliding over her hips, lifting her to him, his thighs thrust between hers, widening them further still. His heart was pounding, deafening him, drumming every sense into meltdown. Her hands snaked around his waist, pulling him down towards her as she arched her spine up to him, saying his name, her voice husky and helpless.

'Nikos—now... Oh, God! Now...just *now*—'

He gave her what she was pleading for. With a surge of triumph he thrust into her, deep and deeper yet. She cried out, high-pitched, and just for a second past and present seemed to blur and merge.

She had cried out like that the very first time…
when he had known he must be as gentle as it
was possible for a man to be, taking a woman
from virgin to lover.

Then it was gone, and the roaring fire of sex-
ual passion was consuming him in its furnace,
and he was thrusting and thrusting again, and
then, with another surge of triumph, he felt her
convulse and liquefy around him. He heard
her cry out again…a gasp, a sob…as his heat
flooded her, fusing her to him. Her body was enclosing him, drawing him further in with wave
after wave of breaking pleasure. It was drowning through him, obliterating everything in existence except this moment of absolute release,
absolute consummation, absolute satiation.

How long it lasted he did not know—could
not know, for time had ceased.

Then oblivion receded and his body became
heavy and inert, drained. Chest heaving, he let
his body slacken, felt her arms, warm against
the sudden chill in his muscles, draw him softly
against her, cradling him as his exhausted limbs
became torpid.

He was dimly aware that he could still feel
after-tremors in her body, slowly ebbing away.
Dimly aware that of all the places in all the world
where he might be, here was the only place.
Dimly aware of a heaviness pressing him down,

as if gravity had suddenly quadrupled and there was no strength left in him.

He said her name. It was all he could do.

And then sleep took him.

Calanthe lay with Nikos's sleeping body in her arms. Her own body was still and cold. So very cold.

And yet the night was warm.

She gazed with blank eyes at the white-painted ceiling. A single thought was circling in her head. Pulsing in her stricken limbs now slack and exhausted.

What have I done? Dear God, what have I done?

But she knew the answer. No matter how many times the question circled endlessly in her sleepless brain.

The fire she had let run so fatefully—so fatally—had burned away all sense. But now that fire was cold, cold ash.

Memory swept over her. Not of the night that had just passed, but of nights so long ago.

How many times had she held him like this in the aftermath of passion, his body deep in heavy slumber, still embracing hers? Countless times in that long-ago lost summer. Until the very last time…

But now… Now there was a new last time.
here must be.

Slowly, she pressed her mouth to his sinewed
noulder as he lay half across her, making her
arewell. What she had once thought she had
ith Nik had never truly been at all—nor was
nis true now. Carefully…very carefully…she
ased her body from his, drew herself away. Got
o her feet, swaying slightly, pushing back her
osened tresses, and reached for her discarded
lothes.

And when Homer's rosy-fingered dawn crept
ut over his wine-dark sea beyond the pebbled
each she had already gone.

Leaving Nikos to wake alone.

CHAPTER SEVEN

'I WAS THINKING, PAPA, of perhaps heading back to London a little earlier than planned,' Calanthe ventured tentatively.

She eyed her father across the dinner table. She'd arrived back in Athens before lunch, having taken the first ferry of the morning, terrified that Nikos would wake and come after her. But she'd made it back home, had heard nothing from him since, and all she could feel was abjectly grateful.

Her father paused in the act of raising his wine glass.

'Oh, my darling girl, why?'

There was dismay in his voice and Calanthe felt doubly bad. She didn't want to leave her father early. Especially right now. She frowned, her eyes resting on him.

Her gaze skimmed his face. He'd told her he'd be cutting back on the rich food, reducing his intake of wine and alcohol in general, but she'd seen no sign of it yet. Tonight's dinner was rich roast lamb, the wine heavy and plentiful. His colour was high, and her announcement just now had made his cheeks flush more. She wanted to ask him—yet again—whether he'd made an appointment for the further tests that he'd admitted his cardiologist had recommended. But he always waved the question away, getting tetchy and irritated, changing the subject determinedly.

Well, tonight the subject was changed, all right. And clearly it wasn't one he welcomed.

'I've a lot to get on with,' she said, hoping he wouldn't ask for details.

His shrewd gaze rested on her and Calanthe wished it wouldn't. She braced herself for his questioning, yet it did not come. Instead, his expression changed, became bland.

'Well, stay at least until next weekend,' he said. 'I had in mind a dinner party for this coming Friday.'

He mentioned some familiar names of his own generation. None, Calanthe thought thankfully, with sons who might make potential husbands for her.

I can last out till the weekend. And if Nikos tries to make contact, then...

She would give instructions that no call from him should be put through, and she would bury

herself at the museum till Friday and stay totally
out of circulation.

Above all, she must not think about the insan
ity she'd committed. Must not feel...must not re
member. Because what else was it except insanity

It could be nothing else. A moment of self
indulgence...succumbing to the soft music an
the velvet night, to the bliss of feeling his arm
around her once more after so long, to his lips or
hers... To the fire he set running in her veins, t
all that she had once had and had never though
could be hers again.

It had been a final chance to take and tast
and claim all that she had once thought migh
be hers for ever.

From a man who had never been the ma
she'd thought he was.

That was all she had to remember. Not tha
night of madness in his arms that she shoul
never, never have allowed...

Nikos glanced up at the imposing building tha
housed the headquarters of Georgios Petrana
kos' property empire, in the business suburb o
Marousi, close to Kifissia.

He'd been summoned there to a meeting.

OK, 'summoned' had not been the word use
by Georgios's efficient-sounding PA. 'Gracious

invited' fitted the bill better. But it was a summons for all that.

And Nikos was very, very interested in knowing why.

There could, he well knew, be any number of reasons. But there was only one he wanted it to be.

He felt his solar plexus clench as he swung through the glass revolving doors into the air-conditioned lobby, giving his name at the reception desk.

He could see the receptionist glance at him appreciatively from under her eyelashes. Normally he would have bestowed a winning smile upon her—after all, why not? But today he refrained for two reasons. One because of the tension building up inside him as to why Georgios had asked him to come and see him, and another reason far more compelling.

Because the very attractive receptionist could, for all he noticed, be as boot-faced as a harpy.

Women no longer existed for him.

Apart from one.

Emotion roiled in him like bilgewater in the hull of a boat, weighing him down. Destabilising him. Words stabbed at him. Cutting into his flesh. Drawing blood.

She walked out on me.

Stark, brutal words. Stabbing again.

She'd walked out after everything that night at the beach house had brought—after the passion and desire, after he'd won her to him, after her body had yielded to his more than ever he remembered, after the sensual bliss that had possessed them both, after he had folded her trembling body against his, his heart hammering, holding her close, so close...

To wake in a cold, empty bed.

The pre-dawn beach house had been chill. Deserted. Silent. At first, with a grabbing of hope, he'd thought she might be in the attached shower room, but that had been deserted too. So had the pebbled beach when he'd yanked open the door.

Then, staring back inside the bleak and silent beach house, he'd realised, with a blow to his guts, that her gown was no longer carelessly thrown over a chair...was no longer visible at all. Only his own crumpled and tossed aside evening clothes cascaded on to the floor, his dress shoes kicked off at the foot of the bed.

She'd gone.

Now only one question burned in his head. Consuming him like a fire within, giving him no peace, no rest.

How do I get her back?

Because getting her back was vital. That night with her—that unforgettable night when he'd rediscovered everything he had ever wanted and so much more—had focussed his entire world on a single name.

Calanthe.

I want her. I want her back. I want her again. I want her in every way. I want her in my life. For my life.

It should have come as a shock for him to realise that, yet it did not. Because it seemed, quite simply, like the truth. Simple, straightforward, obvious. That unforgettable night with her had made that truth undeniable.

All he had to do now was find out how to achieve it.

He stepped into the executive lift that would whisk him straight up to Georgios's office.

And by the time he left his dark eyes were glittering and the set of his mouth was aslant with satisfaction.

'Calanthe, my dear, how well you look. Glowing as ever!'

The compliment coming her way was undeserved. Calanthe knew that despite her carefully applied make-up her cheeks were wan, her colour pale. But she smiled appropriately, greeting the wife of one of her father's oldest friends, then turning to greet the next arrivals for the dinner party.

It would be slightly unbalanced in numbers, for her father had told her that the sister of one of his married guests was visiting Athens and had been included in the invitation. But they would be just under a dozen at the table, and since all the guests knew each other as well as they knew her father, Calanthe envisaged that her role would be minimal. She would probably slip away once coffee had been served in the salon after dinner, and leave her father's generation to their own amusements.

With everyone present, and pre-dinner drinks consumed, dinner itself was announced, and she led the way through to the dining room. She gave a little frown. An extra place had been set. She was about to murmur to the staff that it should be removed when she heard the front door opening again. Heard a voice she would have paid a year's salary—paid any amount—not to hear again.

Her eyes flew to her father. Dismay flooded her, as realisation did likewise. This was his doing—*his*! But he was busy settling the guest on his right-hand side, paying her no attention. Paying no attention to the arrival of this latest extra guest until he walked in.

And then: 'Ah, my boy, I'm so glad you could make it! Such short notice... Come, come—here is your place.' He smiled genially, encompassing both Nikos Kavadis and his daughter. 'You two young people!' he said, beaming, and gestured that Nikos should take the seat next to Calanthe.

There was nothing she could do. Nothing
short of throwing a fit, or fainting, or simply
charging out of the room, grabbing her hand-
bag and her passport and heading for the airport
to take the last flight that night to London—or
anywhere else in the entire world that was not
her father's house in Athens, with Nikos Kava-
lis sitting next to her for dinner.

Frozen with numbness, she lowered herself
jerkily into her chair. Nikos paused while she
seated herself, then sat down beside her.

He turned to her with a smile.

Bland. Unreadable.

And it cut her like a knife.

She hadn't known he'd be here. That was obvious. She looked as if she were about to pass
out on the spot. As he smiled at her, two spots
of hectic colour burned in her whitened cheeks.

'So we meet again,' he said pleasantly, shaking out his linen napkin.

She didn't answer—only swallowed. Everyone around the table continued to chatter, their
conversation easy and convivial. Obviously, all
the guests knew each other well.

A sudden memory shafted through him. That
first evening in the taverna, when he'd inserted
himself into the throng of students spending their
summer vacation excavating the site beside the

resort where he had been working as a builder. The crowd there had been chattering and convivial, easy-going and sociable, welcoming him in.

All except Calanthe.

She'd tried to freeze him out.

Just as she would now, if she could.

But that wasn't going to be possible, was it? Not at her father's dinner table, in the middle of all his guests.

The woman at his left was addressing him, and he turned his attention to her, smiling politely, and answering what she'd asked about who he was, and how he knew Georgios.

And his daughter.

'So nice of Georgios to have invited you for her!' The woman smiled. A glint of open curiosity showed in her eyes. 'Dear Calanthe...always so many admirers! But no one *special* as yet,' she trilled.

The question hung in the air. Athens was a hotbed of gossip. And gossip could be a powerful engine sometimes.

Nikos smiled. 'As yet,' he echoed.

The woman's glint came again. 'Ah! So we must hope...' she trailed openly. 'I know just how much Georgios longs for the dear girl to settle down and finally make her choice. My own son married last year, and my daughter is engaged. It's such a comfort to any parent, but for Georgios, without a son to take over...well, of course, Calanthe's eventual choice will be *so* important—don't you agree?'

'Indeed,' agreed Nikos dutifully, on cue.

He changed the subject, politely asking what line her son was in—he was a commercial property lawyer, it seemed, and her daughter worked for a management consultancy.

'Their father and I are so very proud of their achievements!' the woman enthused. 'They've had to work very hard to get where they are today!'

Nikos veiled his eyes. Memory overwhelmed him again. How, unlike the children of wealthy parents such as these, he'd had to put in long working days during every university vacation, evenings too during term time, earning money to fund his studies.

Working his way through university had not been sufficient, though, to see him right to the end of his long architectural qualifications.

He'd needed extra help.

And he'd got it...

He cleared his thoughts, made some remark about all professions being crowded, and asked what law firm her son worked at. He was conscious that, at his side, Calanthe was conversing with the male guest on her right. Her voice sounded strained, though, her answers stilted.

But it was not her voice he was most conscious of. It was her closeness to him. Her dress was long-sleeved, in a dark blue, with a modest neckline, and she was adorned with a pearl necklace and stud earrings, her hair in its customary upswept style. Just right for a sedate dinner party with her father's friends. But, sedate though her appearance might be, it still had the power to overwhelm his senses, inflame them... to fill him with longing for her.

As they ate, he could feel from time to time the edge of her wide sleeve brush against the sleeve of his jacket. Could catch her perfume, light and floral. Her closeness was a torment—and a temptation. It was tantalising, testing to the limit his iron self-control, being so close to her and yet behaving as if their incandescent night together had never happened. As if he were nothing more than a polite dinner guest in her father's house.

Well, he was going to be more—far more!—than that. Now, thanks to Georgios, he had the green light to go ahead. To take Calanthe into his life.

All he had to do was convince her of it...

And in that he would succeed.

He must, for his happiness depended on it.

Someone across the table asked him something about his business, and then Georgios asked how his dealings with the government officials were going. Conversation became general, focussing on business and politics—things that Nikos had learnt how to handle with ease and confidence. He was, after all, despite his origins, one of them now. Worth a fortune, just as they were.

His glance went to Georgios, veiled again as he remembered what had been discussed in his office. And why…

At his side, Calanthe was silent, focussing on her meal. It was a very rich duck casserole, and he was aware she was only picking at it. She wasn't touching her wine either. Georgios, however, was enjoying himself heartily, beckoning for a refill of his wine glass.

Nikos frowned. Georgios's colour was high, his breathing heavy as he conversed convivially with his friends. As if in slow motion, Nikos saw it happen. Saw Georgios stall, his hand suddenly going to his chest, his wine glass falling to the table. A gasp broke from him and Nikos saw his hand clench over his chest. His heart. Saw him start to keel over sideways.

Nikos was on his feet in seconds, yelling for someone to phone an ambulance as he took Georgios's heavy, slumping weight, lowering him unconscious to the floor to try and take the pressure off his labouring heart which was trying to pump blood to his brain. Cries of consternation were all around, but Nikos only ripped open the front of Georgios's shirt, desperately feeling for a heartbeat.

Then Calanthe was there, crouched down on the other side of her father, whose eyes had now rolled back. Her face was contorted in terror and she clutched at her father's hand.

'There's a pulse,' Nikos said, his voice strained. 'But it's faint.'

'The ambulance is on its way,' someone said, and handed him a phone so he could talk to the emergency call handler about what best to do till it arrived.

It seemed to take an eternity, but then the paramedics were there, taking over. Getting Georgios on a stretcher, then whisking him away in a wail of sirens.

Nikos turned to Calanthe, who'd staggered to her feet and was now swaying, white-faced.

'I'll come with you to the hospital,' he said.

He took her hand. It was as cold as ice.

Nikos was in San Francisco, giving a presentation at a seismology and civil planning conference, but his mind was seven thousand miles away in Athens—where Georgios Petranakos was recuperating from the triple bypass that had been performed after his emergency admission to hospital. His coronary arteries were shot to pieces. Recovery was proving slow.

He had not heard that from Calanthe—had not heard *anything* from her—but from Georgios's finance director. The fact that he was telling Nikos was significant. As were the implications to be drawn from it.

The conference over, and some useful business meetings attended in the Bay area, he returned to Zurich, put in hand an array of measures that would enable him to be absent from his desk for a good while, then flew down to Athens.

He would wait no longer.

'Papa, won't you consider that convalescent home the cardiologist recommended? Being there would help get you back on your feet, with careful exercise and therapy.'

Calanthe tried to make her tone persuasive, but it did not seem to be working. Even though he'd been discharged from hospital, there was a new weariness in her father, and she did not think it was just because he was still recovering—slowly—from major heart surgery. His eyes were sunken, his cheeks hollow.

She felt anxiety nip at her. It reminded her, painfully, of how she'd tried to rally her mother in her final days, intent on keeping her going, not letting her succumb to the dreaded disease gradually taking her over from the inside.

It had been a losing battle...

But this battle for her father must not be lost! There was no reason for it to be lost. Many men survived bypass surgery well—he would too, surely?

Her father shook his head. He seemed fretful, as if he was waiting for something, but she knew not what.

He looked at her, eyes searching. 'Are you going back to London sometime?' he asked.

She shook her head. 'I've taken indefinite compassionate leave,' she said. 'I want to see you well first.'

'What are you doing this evening?' her father asked, as if her assurance that she would not be leaving Athens any time soon was what he'd wanted to hear. 'Anything nice?'

'Yes,' she said, trying to rally him. 'I'm having dinner with you, Papa.'

He made an impatient sound in his throat.

'You should go out!' he said. 'Night after night you are in...'

'Of course I am,' she said. 'I wouldn't dream of abandoning you!'

'I have staff to look out for me—and that nurse you insisted on!' he said. 'But you—you should be out and about. Choosing a man to marry.'

Calanthe's heart sank, but her father was speaking still.

'I've had my warning!' he told her. 'The next attack could finish me off.'

'Oh, Papa don't speak like that!' she said immediately.

He ignored her. 'So I want it settled! Is that too much to ask?'

Calanthe looked at him in consternation. He was not putting this on. He had never been manipulative of her in such a way—had never used emotional blackmail on her.

'Papa—' she began, dismay in her voice. And then broke off. What could she say to him? What could she possibly say when what he wanted was impossible?

The house phone on her bedside table was ringing and Calanthe picked it up. Her earlier conversation with her father was still in her head, fretting at her. The voice at the other end of the line wiped it from her thoughts.

'Before you hang up on me, listen—please.'

Nikos's voice was brisk and businesslike. That, and that alone, kept her on the line.

'Well?' she replied, her voice tight.

'I want you to have dinner with me.'

Her hand clenched over the handset. 'Are you mad?'

'Far from it.' The brisk, businesslike tones were clear down the line. 'There's a matter I need to discuss with you.' There was an infinitesimal pause. 'It concerns your father.'

She stiffened even more. 'In what way?'

'I shall discuss that with you over dinner.'

He gave the name of the restaurant, set the time, and rang off.

Calanthe stared at the phone in her hand, then slowly lowered it.

Conscious that she could hear the thud of her heart.

Hating it that she could.

The restaurant Nikos had chosen was quiet, and discreet. Warily, Calanthe took a seat at the table as he stood up at her approach. He was in a superbly tailored charcoal lounge suit, with a dark grey tie. Every inch the businessman. Not the lover. It might have reassured her, but it didn't. She herself had dressed sombrely, in an olive-green dress with a high neckline and no jewellery.

She had not seen Nikos since that fateful dinner party where her father had nearly died. Why had he asked her here?

That was the question she put to him once the waiters had left them alone, after fussing endlessly, it seemed to Calanthe, with menus and iced water and bread rolls and wine lists.

His answer, when he disclosed his reason, froze her in disbelief.

CHAPTER EIGHT

'YOU WOULD BE doing it for your father,' Nikos heard his own voice saying.

'Would I?' Calanthe's tone was scathing.

'There would be other reasons, too.'

His eyes rested on her. Her face had closed, her mouth was pinched, and her eyes were steely.

'Really? You mean apart from handing my father's company to you on a plate.' She gave an acid smile that didn't alter the expression on her face. 'And myself as well.'

He lifted his glass to his mouth. Felt himself relax.

'It is what your father wants,' he said smoothly. 'You surely know that.'

Her face stayed rigid. Then she cut to the chase.

'Why you?'

He eased his knife through the tender fillet of chicken, cut himself a slice.

'He believes me capable of running his com pany...finding synergies with my own, to ou mutual advantage.' He paused. 'He spelt it ou quite clearly to me when he all but interviewe me for the role the week of that dinner party.'

Her eyes were gimlets. 'Which role would tha be? CEO or son-in-law?' Again, her words wer acid.

'Both.' He forked up the chicken. 'That's th whole point, Calanthe.'

He let his eyes rest on her again. Rejection ra diated from her like a force field. It might hav been a sign to be taken negatively, but he kne\ it for the opposite. Knew why she was radiatin rejection on all frequencies.

A small smile formed briefly at his mouth a he watched her bristle like a porcupine at hi words. Her sole was barely touched, her utensi gripped in nerveless hands.

'You saw at that dinner party with his frienc and peers how acceptable the notion was to him he went on. 'How expected. It was always goin to be so—one day his daughter would marr suitably, and his son-in-law would carry his bus ness forward.'

He tilted an eyebrow.

'You have no interest in doing so—he mac that clear to me—and he also made clear I would have welcomed it had you done so. But he respects your choice of career. However…'

He paused again, his gaze levelling with hers.

'He will not willingly see his life's work discontinued. Without a competent and suitable son-in-law, after his days have passed, the assets would be disposed of and the company either liquidated or sold on. No matter how much money that would leave you with, what he has spent his life building up would be dissipated. He does not want that. Hence this solution. It suits everyone all round.'

Her eyes narrowed. 'Except me,' she said.

Nikos's expression changed, his eyelids half veiling his gaze. 'You say that to me after our night together?' he said.

There was a caress in his voice, he knew. A promise.

Her knife and fork clattered to the tablecloth. Her head shot back. 'That night should never have happened. Never!'

He held her gaze without concession. There had been something more in it than repudiation—something revealing.

She cannot deny what our night together brought her! What it meant for her…for both of us…

He had to make her see it and accept it. Accept everything that went with it. Everything he had brought her here to accept.

'But it did, Calanthe—it did happen. And it proved just how good we are together—deny it all you will! I told you there, on the beach, how important you were becoming to me, and now—'

A choke broke from her.

He did not let it stop him.

'Now I have the chance to tell you again...to tell you how...how special you have become to me. Eight years ago you were too young, and I had my way to make in the world. The time was not right for us. But now, Calanthe, *now* the time *is* right. So very right.'

His voice was a caress again. He wanted, *needed* her to accept what he was telling her.

'Had your father not collapsed as he did, I would have taken the time to woo you properly... win you over to me. But your father needs the reassurance we can give him now. Would you begrudge him that?'

She stared across at him, her face still closed. 'It's not him I begrudge,' she said. Her voice was tight, her mouth pinched.

He reached his hand across the table. Touched her fingers with his. Leant towards her. Her face was still leaden, and he didn't want it that way.

He didn't want words like bullets, the freezing off and the rejection. He didn't want that at all.

He wanted the woman he'd led down that scented pathway to the private darkness of the beach house…the woman he'd taken into his arms, her body aflame for him, trembling with a desire that answered his own, surging in his body, urging his possession of her.

He felt desire quicken in him again now, as his hand closed over hers, felt hers beneath it.

His voice was low once more when he spoke again. 'What is between us—what has *always* been between us—cannot be denied! Be honest with yourself. Be honest with me as I am honest with you.'

Something came into her eyes. A flash. Dark like black lightning. Had he really seen it? Or had it been a trick of the light?

He felt her hand drawing back from his, withdrew his own.

Frustration filled him and made him speak more bluntly than he wanted. 'Calanthe, this would protect your father! He just isn't well enough to go back into harness. His heart is weakened—you cannot want to risk another attack! Not when it is so easy for you to remove that risk.'

He saw his warning hit home…pressed further. 'When he outlined his hopes to me he told me about your mother, Calanthe. That she had died far too young. Deprived of old age. Don't let that happen to your father too. Not when it would be so easy to prevent it.'

For one long last moment he let his gaze rest on her, met her veiled, oblique regard of him. Then she spoke, with no expression in her voice.

'I'd like to go home now, Nikos,' she said. 'No, don't get up. I'll get a taxi. Finish your dinner. I'm sorry I only picked at mine.'

She got to her feet, walked stiffly away, as though tension racked her body. He watched her leave the restaurant, then sat back, unconsciously reaching for his wine glass. He caught the lingering fragrance of her perfume. All that was left of her presence there.

What will she decide?

He did not know.

Knew only that there was only one answer he could bear to hear from her.

'Your father is asking for you,' the housekeeper informed Calanthe as she stepped through the doorway.

Calanthe bit her lip. The last thing she could face right now was seeing her father. Her brain was in meltdown, churning with thoughts, emotions and feelings that she could not process, that had turned her upside down and inside out.

I didn't see it coming.

But it had—like a bomb exploding inside her.

She hurried up the stairs, knowing she must face her father—but not, dear God, with the true extent of her feelings.

Not that I even know what they are. I'm all in pieces—completely in pieces!

Her father was in bed, and the massive bed frame was dwarfing him, she realised with a pang, as it had never done previously. He looked frail and ill. The pang in her heart struck more deeply, but she put a cheerful smile on her face, moving across to kiss his sunken cheek.

'How are you feeling?' she asked brightly.

'That depends on you,' came the laboured reply. 'You have been to dinner with young Karadis? Of course I knew! He asked my permission first! So...' he levelled his sunken eyes on her '...what answer have you given him?'

Dismay flushed through her. She could see in his eyes what she did not want to see. Expectation...and hope.

She felt her stomach clench.

'Papa, I—' Her mouth was dry suddenly. 'It... it was...out of the blue.'

She sounded like a Victorian maiden, she thought wildly, trotting out the traditional *Oh, this is so sudden!* prevarication.

The expression in her father's eyes changed.

It was knowing now—amused, even. As though his daughter was an open book to him. And Nikos too.

'Really?' he riposted sceptically. 'The man hasn't been able to take his eyes off you! Right from when he walked into my party! Do you think I can't tell when a man has been struck by lightning? Oh, you may play the ice queen,' he said, the amusement deepening, 'but that can be alluring to a man like him. He's a man who knows what he wants. He's made himself something from nothing—achieved everything he wanted. And now...' his eyes rested on Calanthe and she could not escape their message '...he wants you.'

She felt her face tighten. 'What he *wants*, Papa, is your company!' she bit out.

He waved his hand again. 'Of course he does! I would not respect him if he didn't!' His voice changed, and there was shrewdness in his face once more. 'And I would not contemplate him coming within a hundred metres of it if I didn't think he had three essential qualities. One— ambition. The way *I* had it, Calanthe, when I started out in business. The kind of ambition to make something of myself—as he has already proved he has. The second is competence. I will not let what I have spent my life building up be in the hands of someone who isn't capable. And the third…'

Calanthe saw his expression change, soften. 'The third is obvious.'

He held his hand out to her. Automatically she took it, feeling its warmth, its cherishing. A lump rose in her throat.

'He will make a good husband for you, *pethi mou*. Truly he will. To him, you are a prize in yourself—not just because you are my daughter! He values you as a man *should* value the woman he marries.'

He shut his eyes for a moment, then opened them again. Naked longing was clear in them for her to see.

'It's all I want for you, my darling, dearest daughter. To see you settled and happy. With a man who is worthy of you.'

She heard his words. Felt ice pool in her stomach.

Worthy.

Nikos Kavadis was 'worthy' of her…

The ice in her stomach chilled even more.

She felt her father squeeze her hand, then release it. He looked tired suddenly, and weary, and ill. The lump in her throat thickened, and fear clutched at her. What if he never recovered from his bypass? What if his ailing heart failed again? This time for ever…

Ice pooled in her again—but not because o
Nikos.

'I just long to see you settled,' her father said
again, and in his voice there was longing and
hope—and fear. Fear that she might not, no
even now, when he was lying there, stricken
and frail, his brush with death narrowly es
caped.

Heaviness filled her, and a sense of the room
closing in on her. It left nothing but herself, sit
ting on her father's bed, looking at his face filled
with all that he wanted for her.

Slowly, she got to her feet. 'I know, Papa,
know,' she said softly.

Love was in her eyes, and pity too—and an
guish.

She bent to kiss his cheek, to murmur good
night to him. But as she turned and left the room
there was something else in her eyes.

Resolve.

And the heaviness inside her was like a con
crete weight. Dragging her to the bottom of th
sea. The deep and drowning sea...

Nikos sat at the desk in his hotel room, attemp
ing to focus his thoughts on own business a
fairs. But he hadn't touched the keyboard on h
laptop for ten minutes.

Since she'd left him at dinner last night the

had been nothing from Calanthe. Nor from Georgios Petranakos either. He would give it another twenty-four hours, then head back to Zurich.

But every atom of his being resisted such action.

He stared at the blank wall in front of him, feeling emotions shift and shape within him.

Surely Calanthe would accept him? And not just for her father's sake, but for her own too? Surely now she would finally let the past go? Would accept what had brought them back together after so long? How much he wanted her and she him?

Longing filled him. Memories of that night at the beach house tormented him.

Waking to an empty bed had been unbearable.

All I want is her—Calanthe.

Her name rang in his head.

A ping sounded from his laptop—an email arriving. Another one. He'd ignored most of them, his mind too distracted to pay them any attention. But he cast a cursory glance down to see who this one was from and suddenly his entire attention was on it.

It was from Calanthe.

He clicked it open. Conscious that his heart rate had increased. Conscious that he resented the fact that it had. Conscious that he did not know how to predict just what her answer would be. Or even if she was prepared to give it.

It seemed she was.

The email was brief.

I accept.

Yes! He wanted to punch the air in triumph.

Then, just below, in parentheses, he saw she'd written something else.

(Ts and Cs apply. To be discussed and confirmed.)

He didn't care. He snatched up his phone, to call the Petranakos mansion immediately, but before he could the hotel phone rang.

He wanted to ignore it, but didn't.

'Yes?' His tone was impatient.

It was Calanthe.

'Nikos?' She sounded brisk. Businesslike, even. 'You have my email now. Meet me for lunch in forty-five minutes.'

She named a restaurant, and the street it was on.

He frowned. That was the same street as Petranakos HQ. But he made no demur—only agreed. He made no mention of her email, or what it contained, making his voice smooth and co-operative.

'Of course. I'll see you there.'

She rang off and he sat back. That sense of triumph was still coursing through him.

Triumph—and more than triumph.

A sense of achievement so intense it filled him completely.

It was like déjà vu, Calanthe thought as she sat down at the table in the restaurant she'd stipulated. But this time she wasn't going to be sideswiped. For a start, she was at the restaurant first. Secondly, she was well briefed this time around.

As Nikos would discover.

She ordered an elderflower spritzer from the hovering waiter, who was being very attentive, knowing she was the daughter of one of their most regular patrons, and then settled back to watch for Nikos's arrival.

He turned up dead on time, making straight for her table, wearing the same darkly formidable charcoal business suit and grey tie as he had the previous night. It had the same impact on her—the one she didn't want it to have but could not prevent. She felt her hands clench in her lap. Well, she must, that was all. Too much depended on it.

An image hung in her mind of the way her father had reached for her hand last night, his frailty tugging at her, her love for him squeezing her heart.

Nikos sat himself down, smiled pleasantly at her, greeted her civilly. But his expression was unreadable. The waiter was there again, and Calanthe noted that Nikos had ordered a martini. Dry—but potent. It gave her the slight sense of an edge over him. An edge she would need, she knew.

For the next few minutes there was the business of menus, and ordering, and iced water, and bread rolls, but finally they were left to themselves. It was a relatively early lunch, so the restaurant was quiet.

Nikos glanced at her. 'Why this particular restaurant?' he asked. 'I'd have happily come out to Kifissia…met you somewhere there.'

It was a leading question, and Calanthe acknowledged it.

'It was the most convenient,' she said. 'I've just spent the morning with my father's financial director.'

If Nikos was surprised, he hid it.

'He seems a sound man,' he commented.

She knew he'd already met the man, and that her father had introduced him to several of the other senior directors. Nikos would have wanted

meet the executive team—there was no way
e could step into Georgios's shoes on any other
erms. He would have to show himself to be ap-
roving of the calibre of the senior executives,
nd, indeed, agree to co-operate with them.

Calanthe nodded. She knew her father's FD
ersonally, as a frequent dinner guest with his
vife, along with several other board members.
ut her meeting with him that morning had been
f a specific nature. So had her conversation
ith her father earlier that day.

'I've also talked to my father,' she said now.
he looked straight across at Nikos. 'I wanted
o be sure I understand exactly the terms on
vhich you will be taking the burden of running
is company from him—and,' she added point-
dly, 'what his senior team think of it. Also, cru-
ially...' she held Nikos's unrevealing gaze '...
vhat they think of you.'

Nikos's martini arrived, and he took a rumi-
ative sip as the waiter glided away.

'And...?' he posed to Calanthe.

She took a breath. 'It seems both my father's
otion, and you yourself, are deemed sound,'
he said.

'I'm glad to see you reassured,' Nikos said.

His voice was smooth. Too smooth for her liking.

She took a mouthful of her spritzer, for her
iouth was suddenly dry. She was doing her

level best to be Little Miss Cool, but her senses kept trying to distract her. Kept trying to get her gaze to fix on just what it was about him that seemed to quicken the blood in her veins, make her heart beat faster. But she had to stay cool.

'However, I did tell my father, and his senior team, that if we go ahead with my father's plan I will join the board.'

Nikos stilled. She saw it. Felt it giving her an edge again. He hadn't seen that coming.

'I may not be a born businesswoman, but I won't totally abstain from any degree of responsibility or commitment. I want a seat on the board, so that I am involved in some capacity. My father and his team have no objection,' she said pointedly.

She watched Nikos pick up his martini again, revolve the glass slowly in his fingers.

'You want to keep an eye on me?' he said.

She nodded. *Because you've got previous, Nik...*

He cocked an eyebrow at her. 'Any other Ts and Cs on your list?'

For a second, Calanthe could not stop her expression hardening. Yes, she had some more—but she would not disclose them now. Not yet. Not till the time was right.

She felt Nikos's gaze narrow assessingly. She made her expression relax. 'Some more may

occur to me, but for now that's it. After all...'
she looked at him straight '...right now we're
only talking about an engagement. Nothing is
fixed until we marry and you sign whatever paperwork my father has had drawn up for you.'

He sat back, lifting his martini glass, eyes
resting on her. 'Thinking of jilting me at the
altar?' he said casually.

Was there humour in his voice? Baiting? Teasing, even?

She wouldn't rise to it. She was feeling a
sense of relief—a reaction to the tension that had
gripped her since he'd walked up to the table—
and now the effect of his physical presence was
there again, impacting her, overwhelming her,
making her blood kick, her breath quicken...
mixing memory and desire...

No!

Slamming down on that oh-so-dangerous
word, she said instead, 'No altar, Nikos. A civil
wedding only.'

He frowned. 'Won't your father want the full
works?'

'Let's keep this simple, Nikos,' she said.

Her voice was low. She felt the tremble in it.
A tremble she didn't want. Her eyes dropped to
the tablecloth.

Suddenly, she felt her arm being touched. The
briefest gesture on her bare forearm.

'Calanthe…' she heard him say. His voice wa soft. Almost tender.

She looked up, blinking. He was gazing a her—openly so. She couldn't bear it…but she could not look away.

'You will not regret this,' he said. 'I have rushed you, I know, because of your father's ill ness. But even if I cannot woo you properly be fore our wedding, I will woo you after.'

His smile was a caress, a promise…

She felt colour beat up in her—and heat. Hi eyes, so dark, so drowning, were telling her how beautiful he found her, how desirable, how h could not resist her…

Nor could she resist him.

She heard herself speak. A mere breath of ai Saying his name. 'Nikos…' A sigh, an exhalatio

Heat flushed her body, filling it with longing with desire. He took her hand, cradled it in his. Hi eyes didn't leave her. He turned her hand over in hi and then, the tender skin of her inner wrist exposed drew it to his mouth. Grazed its silken surface wit his lips. Weakness drowned through her…

'Mademoiselle…'

It was the waiter, arriving with their firs courses.

She yanked her hand away, cheeks burning Nikos gave a low laugh, leaning back as th waiter deposited his *assiette*, having bestowed Calanthe's upon her.

'Is there anything else?' the waiter asked politely.

Nikos glanced up at him. 'A glass of champagne for each of us,' he announced.

As the waiter murmured his assent, Nikos's glance turned to Calanthe. 'To celebrate,' he said.

The waiter glided away, and Nikos reached inside his jacket, drawing out a small, distinctive box, flicking it open.

'And not just with champagne,' he murmured. His gaze rested on her, sending a message to her, along with the contents of the box. A message it was impossible for her to deny—though it made her own gaze veil, her throat tighten suddenly.

Calanthe's eyes dropped to the ring he was placing in front of her. The diamond solitaire—worth a fortune, she knew—glittered at her, its message clear. Nikos, staking his claim to her.

Re-claiming her, after eight long years...

And never, *never*, had it rung so bitter.

So achingly hollow...

The wedding was to be as quiet as Calanthe could make it.

She wanted minimum stress on her father.

And on herself.

Her mind slid sideways, as it had been doing

ever since she had sent that fateful email of acceptance to Nikos.

A feeling of complete unreality had settled over her as she'd gone through the motions required for organising the civil wedding she'd insisted on.

Despite her father's objections she'd held adamant on that point. She'd also been adamant that no announcement at all would be made of the forthcoming wedding. She would, she'd informed her father, tell their friends afterwards, justifying her decision by revealing her father's ill health.

There was one other thing she had remained adamant about. Nikos had moved out of his hotel and into a rented flat, near enough to both Marousi and Kiffisia, but he would live in it on his own until the wedding. Calanthe had been crystal-clear about that.

'My father will expect it,' she told Nikos. 'And nor do I want to leave him at this time, while he is still so weak.'

Nikos hadn't liked it—but had gone along with it. Besides, he'd been busy too, she knew. He was running his own company remotely—albeit with one quick trip back to Zurich—and immersing himself in the running of her father's company too.

She, too, had alterations to make in her life.

She knew she would have to give up her job in London…see if she could take up full-time work of a comparable nature here in Athens.

Keeping busy had helped. Helped her stop thinking about what she was doing. Helped her stop thinking about Nikos.

She was holding him at bay, she knew. And she knew why too. She was keeping their time together at a minimum, citing her own desire to spend as much time with her father as she could before moving out of his home. Again, Nikos hadn't liked it—but had gone along with it.

His words from the lunch where she had given in to what he wanted echoed in her head.

'…*if I cannot woo you properly before our wedding, I will woo you after…*'

She pulled her mind away. She could not think about 'after' until it came.

Nikos said the words he needed to say. Heard Calanthe say hers. Heard the officiant speak his part.

Apart from the necessary witnesses and officials, the only other person present at Kifissia's town hall was Georgios Petranakos. Drawn and ill as he still was, there was a look on the older man's face that was one of satisfaction. Relief.

It was something Nikos could echo—and far more intensely.

Finally, Calanthe was his!

Eight years ago he'd left her—

His thoughts pulled away from the memory like a plane hitting turbulence.

But now…

Now I will never walk away again.

Emotion welled within him, inchoate but powerful. He did not know what it was—only that it made him turn and look at her now, feeling it rise within him again, catching at his lungs.

How much she moved him!

Just to look at her was a delight.

She wore a simple cream dress, narrow-cut, knee-length, and with cap sleeves. Expensive, obviously, but not showy—discreetly elegant. Also low-heeled court shoes and pearls at her ears and throat, with her hair in a coiled chignon set with pearl combs. Her make-up was subtle, but enhanced her natural beauty. In her hands was a small bouquet of cream-coloured flowers, delicately scented, hand-tied with cream satin ribbons.

Nikos's breath caught again as he felt that strange emotion well up in him once more. She looked, he thought, like perfection itself.

The slightest frown formed between his brows.

But her expression was grave…tense, even.

He gave a forbearing mental shake. Well, that was to be expected. She had nearly lost her father—

his health was still a major concern to her—and she had been rushed into marriage because of it.

His words to her—the promise that he had made when she had finally accepted the necessity of their rapid marriage—came back to him.

He had, indeed, had no time to woo her.

His wooing, as he had promised, would come after their wedding.

He felt anticipation flush through him.

Starting tonight…

The celebrant was speaking again. Solemn, binding words. Uniting them in matrimony. Binding them together—he to her, she to him.

And it was done.

He turned towards her, smiled down at her. She was as pale as her dress, her expression unreadable. But he did not mind. Nerves were understandable on a bride's wedding day.

He murmured her name—a caress in itself. Lowered his head to brush her lips with his.

They were as cold as marble.

Anticipation flared within him. Soon… Ah, soon he would warm those lips. And all that he had rediscovered on that glorious night at the beach house would be theirs again.

He could not wait.

Calanthe kissed her father goodnight. They had dined at home, after the wedding. Her father and

Nikos would have far preferred dining out, but she had put her foot down, claiming it would be too tiring for her father after the exertion of attending the wedding.

It had been a strained affair—both the wedding itself and dinner *à trois*—but she had coped. Most of the conversation over dinner had been between her father and Nikos, and she had been relieved. She had only been able to pick at her food and had hardly touched her wine.

Nerves had racked her, and now, as she bade goodnight to her father, they racked her even more.

She was trying not to think—not to let any thoughts into her head at all. Keeping her mind as blank as she could. Trying, above all, not to let the one question that clamoured to be released pound in her head.

What have I done? Dear God, what have I done?

Because there was no point letting it out.

She knew what she had done.

She had married Nikos Kavadis.

The man who had broken her heart eight years ago was now her husband.

Nikos could feel the tension in him mounting. The car was pulling up outside the modern apartment block…the driver was getting out to open the door for them. He got out first, nodding at the driver, holding out his hand to help Calanthe. She got out without taking it, murmuring her thanks to the driver, then walked to the apartment block entrance.

Nikos dismissed the car, extracting from his jacket pocket the key card that would open the doors for them. They slid aside and he stepped in with Calanthe, the air-con in the lobby chill after the external temperature.

He was glad they were repairing straight to his apartment. There was no need to fuss with wedding nights in flash hotels, and because of Georgios's poor health a honeymoon away right now was out of the question.

Besides, now that he was officially Georgios Petranakos's son-in-law there was a great deal of work to be done in stepping fully into the CEO's shoes. A honeymoon could come later—the Maldives, the Seychelles, maybe even the South Seas...

Until then...

His eyes glinted, his gaze going to Calanthe now as she stood beside him in the elevator. It was carrying another passenger—a neighbour, Nikos presumed—so conversation between himself and Calanthe was absent. They got out at his floor, and Nikos readied the key card.

Calanthe was already familiar with the apartment—he'd brought her here before the wedding to show it to her. He opened the door for her now and she stepped inside. She seemed, he thought on edge. Well, so was he. But his weeks of tortuous self-denial were about to end...

'Coffee?' he said to her now.

It was not what he wanted—there was only one thing he wanted—but he could be patient if she wanted to collapse for a while...put her feet up, knock back a coffee, maybe even linger over a liqueur.

She shook her head. 'Thank you, no,' she said.

There was something different in her voice. Nikos frowned. She was walking through into the large reception room, with its stylish modern furniture. He followed her in, and as he did so she turned.

'I have something to say to you,' she said.

He paused, looking at her. There was something different in her face, too. Something in the set of her shoulders, the lift of her chin.

Out of nowhere, Niko felt his expression change—grow tense.

And then she was speaking. Her voice no longer merely crisp, but cutting like a knife. Slicing to the bone.

Her face was like a stone. 'Whatever you expected of this marriage, Nikos, understand this. It will be a marriage in name only,' she said, and her eyes were like gimlets, sharp and piercing. 'You will not be laying a finger on me.' She drew a breath—a harsh, hard sound, as hard as her expression. 'Not now. Not ever,' she said. '*Never* again.'

Calanthe felt weakness flood through her, debilitating and depleting—the aftermath of the tension that had racked her body from the moment she had sat alone in the car with Nikos.

She had said it—dear God, she had actually said it! Said what she had been waiting to say ever since she had given in to her terror for her father, yielded to what he longed for, what she dared not refuse when his brush with death had come so close and might yet come closer still.

What it had been absolutely essential for her to say had now been said. For Nikos to hear.

What I never wanted to tell him.

He was looking at her as if she were from another planet. She wanted to laugh, but laughter might break her apart, and she had used up all her strength today—the very last of it. She could take no more.

He made a start towards her, but she stepped back, a jerking, instinctive movement, forcing her legs to do so.

Then: 'Why the *hell*,' he said, 'are you saying that?'

The incomprehension in his voice was absolute. She saw his face work.

'Calanthe—what is going on? I know you're tired—exhausted, probably…any wedding day is a strain.' He took a breath—a ragged one. 'Look, you can call it a day, OK? I'll make some coffee and you can take it to bed with you. Have a shower, take your make-up off, get into bed.' He took another breath. 'I'll sleep in the spare room. Give you peace and quiet. Give you space. Give you time.'

She looked at him. Keeping her face like stone. Her eyes like granite. Expressionless. Unyielding.

'You could give me eternity, Nikos, and it wouldn't be enough. You see…' She heard the words coming from her. Words that had been eight years in the making. 'You are the very last man on this earth that I would *ever* soil myself on or let near me again.'

She saw his expression change, his brows snap together.

'Why?' he said bluntly.

His face had closed, like a guillotine slicing down over it.

'Because of what you did eight years ago,' she answered.

Her legs would hardly hold her upright, but she forced them to do so.

His eyes flashed. She could see, as clear as day, that he was veiling what was in them.

He knows—he knows why I've said what I have. I can see it and he cannot hide it from me.

Bitterness filled her. And all the more when he said what he said next.

'Because I ended things with you?'

He was making his voice sound open—but she knew that was the very last thing it was...

'Calanthe, I told you—I said to you that very first day at Cape Sounion why I did it. I thought it was a summer romance only...feared that maybe...'

He drew another breath, keeping his eyes fixed on her. She could see that he wanted her to believe what he was saying.

'Maybe you were reading more into it—it was your first romance, and I knew that. Yes, I regret that I left you so abruptly, but I've explained why. I had to get back to my grandmother. That was the reason I left the island.'

She shut her eyes as if to shut him out of existence. Shut out what he had just trotted out to her.

Then: *'Don't lie to me!'* The words were spat from her. Her hands clenched at her sides. A blinding pain came in her head, making her sway. 'You didn't leave the island because of your grandmother! You didn't leave me because you thought it was just a summer romance!'

Her eyes narrowed to slits. The fury in her now possessed her utterly, in an overpowering tide that had been banked for eight long, endless years. She spoke again, every word deadly. Each one finding its mark.

'You left me, Nikos,' she said, 'for one reason and one reason only.'

Her eyes were like knives. Stabbing right into him.

'Because my father *paid* you to leave me.'

CHAPTER NINE

T WAS SAID. Said in words that could never be unsaid. Words she had stored within herself all these years. That had eaten into her, eaten into the heart she had broken over him. Over a man who had taken her father's money to walk out on her.

Pain twisted inside her like torsion in her guts. He was standing there, stock-still, the blood drained from his face.

She went on speaking, saying what had been buried in the deepest part of her for so long. 'When did you find out who I was?'

Even now she dreaded the answer. Dreaded to hear that he had known all along. That he had seduced her knowingly...

Because if that were so then...

Then she would not even have those precious memories of their time together to cling to.

There was no expression in his face as he answered her. 'When your father's fixers arrived. Just before—just before I left you.'

His voice had no emotion in it—none. And then something dark and deadly flashed in his eyes.

'Calanthe, for God's sake—if you have known all along, why wait till now to throw it at me?'

The words broke from him, raw and uncomprehending.

Her face contorted. 'Confront you with the ultimate humiliation a woman can endure?' Her voice twisted and she had to force the words from her, each one burning like acid in her throat.

It hurts—oh, God, how it hurts! To know what he did... To know that money—my father's money—was more important to him than I was! After all we had together! After he held me in his arms, kissed me, made love to me—laughed with me and held my hands. We were together, a couple, him and me...

But it had meant nothing at all to him.

Nothing.

All that had been important to him was the money her father had offered to get rid of him...

And he'd taken the money.

Condemning himself for ever.

She saw his expression tighten.

Words gritted from him. 'I told your father's fixers that you must never know—'

He broke off.

She could not bear to look at him. Could not bear it.

'No, it's not something you'd want known about yourself! Just what you stooped to!' she shot at him. 'Well, my father told me,' she said flatly. 'He said...he said I needed to know.' There was a stone in her lungs, so that she couldn't breathe. 'That I needed to know I would always be a target for unscrupulous men who would romance me, seduce me, tell me anything I wanted to hear—but whatever they did, whatever they said, all they would want would be his money.'

Her voice was as hollow as his now, her eyes dead. She shifted restlessly, as if moving might untwist the torsion in her guts, but it only tightened it, making it agonising to endure.

'And now his money is what you have again, Nik,' she said, unconsciously using the name she'd called him by all those years ago, when the world had been a wonderful place and Nik the most wonderful man in that wonderful world. 'And much, much more of it this time! By bringing you in to run his company he's made you richer than even you've made yourself. Oh, you'll work for it, I'm sure—hard and well—

and you'll earn your share of the profits tha will accrue now.'

She forced a ragged, razored breath into he stone-filled lungs, forced herself to look at hin He was standing there, so close—and yet so in finitely far away—with shock still immobilisin him. Because what else could he feel but shoc at what she'd thrown at him, that she'd know about him all along, shock that was making h face grey like ash?

'You've told me twice now, Nik, that I ar "important" to you—and I know I am. I alway was, from the minute you knew I was my fa ther's daughter.'

He started forward. 'Calanthe—that's no why! You're important to me because—'

Her hand slashed upwards, silencing hin 'Don't try and make it right, Nik! It cannot b made right! Because *nothing* can justify wh you did! Oh, you might well have left me any way—I know that. That's the line you've tro ted out to me—that it was a summer romanc that I was so young, that you had your way make in the world. But you found a good wa to make it easier for yourself, didn't you? *Did you?* With my father's money. The pay-off y took to walk out on me.'

Bitterness and pain and burning humiliatic consumed her.

'You wanted my father's money. Not me.' She took another razored breath. 'Well, that's what you've got now, too.'

She made herself look at him again. He hadn't moved—not a muscle. Somehow she made herself walk past him, head to the front door of the apartment. There she paused and turned back to him.

'I won't be living with you here, Nikos. I've rented the apartment next door. So far as my father is concerned I'm with you. And the world can think that too. I'll socialise with you, keep up appearances—for my father's sake, you understand. I'll stick this out until he's well enough to hear that we've split up, that I married in haste and repented all too quickly.' Her voice twisted. 'He knows, you see, that I make mistakes when it comes to falling for men. As for his company—well, as I say, I'm sure you'll run it well, and make money both for him and yourself, and everyone will be happy because of it.'

She frowned.

'Not much has changed, has it, Nik? Eight years ago my father paid you to leave me. Now, because he wants you to run his company and be the son-in-law he's been waiting years for, he's paying you to stay with me. He bought you off—now he's buying you in.'

She took a breath…it was a like a razor in her throat.

'Well, enjoy it, Nik—enjoy all the Petranakos money coming your way now. This time around it's all you'll get.'

She pulled open the door, stepped through…

And was gone.

Calanthe watched the lights around Gatwick get closer as the plane descended. She had been desperate to get away, right out of Greece, so she'd walked out of the apartment block and headed for Eleftheriou Airport, taken the first flight to London. She'd land after midnight but she didn't care. She'd head for her flat and take refuge there.

Like a wounded animal…

She closed her eyes, saw that monstrous scene in Nik's apartment playing and replaying in her head. Saw herself throwing at him the accusation that had burned within her for so long, shameful and shaming. The thing that she had *never* wanted to admit to. The ultimate humiliation.

She had turned it into anger—anger that was utterly justified—and condemned him for what he'd done. But it had taken all her strength to face the man who had taken money to leave her, to look him in the eyes and tell him she knew she had been *nothing* to him…

She gave a sob of misery.

I loved him! I loved him with all my stupid, stupid heart!

Her hands twisted in her lap, nails digging into her palms. And now she was facing the worst pain of all. The pain she could not bear to face. But she had to.

If she had never set eyes on Nikos again she might have survived his betrayal eight years ago. But he had walked back into her life with devastating consequences—that night in the beach house, in his arms, finding again the bliss she had once known with him when she had first loved him.

And she knew, with another anguished sob, that she loved him again…

Nikos stood on the balcony of his apartment in Zurich, overlooking the lake. The air off the mountains was cool. Autumn would fall sooner here than in Greece, and then the winter's snows would come. But he already dwelled in the land of winter…the land of perpetual ice and snow. It was a land he had not expected ever to be exiled to. And he might never escape. Not even if—

He cut off his thoughts.

Too dangerous. Far, far too dangerous.

Better to accept the perpetual ice and snow.

It was all he deserved.

His thoughts were bitter, like acid in his throat.

I never wanted her to know. Never wanted her to know what I had done.

But she had known all along. Known even in that moment he'd set eyes on her again, walking up to her at her father's birthday party.

Every time she looked at me she knew.

He stared blindly out over the dark waters of the lake. No wonder she had left him that morning, after their night together in the beach house...the night he had believed had brought them back together again. When all along...

He wrenched his hands from the wooden balustrade, turned sharply away, strode back indoors. He needed a drink. Any drink. Anything at all that might dull the rawness inside him, which felt as if the skin had been torn from his flesh.

He yanked open his cocktail cabinet, splashed out a slug of malt whisky, knocked it back as if it were water. It burned as it went down his throat and he poured another.

But he did not drink it. He put the glass down roughly instead. Felt his jaw set like steel as a thought came to him.

He had one chance—one only.

One hope—one only.

And everything...*everything*...depended on it.

Calanthe was in Berlin, attending a conference on Late Antiquity which her former boss at the

London museum had agreed she could still go
o if she reported back on it. She'd gone straight
rom London, and it would mop up a few days.

She'd emailed her father when she'd arrived
n London, saying she had some loose ends to
ie up in clearing her desk, sorting out her flat
nd bringing over what she would need for a
ermanent stay in Athens.

As for Nikos, she'd simply tersely texted him
o say she was in London. He would know why,
nd that it had nothing to do with what she'd
old her father.

It was simply to avoid him.

He would be busy, anyway, she knew. He had
lot to take over at her father's company, and
e had his own to run as well. He was in Zurich
ight now, and she was glad of it. It would give
er some time in Athens without him.

But she could not avoid him for ever. She
new that. She had meant what she'd said when
he'd told him that she would appear as his
vife in public, for the sake of her father. Yet
he dreaded it with all her being.

To stand beside him…to be Kyria Kavadis, ac-
epting congratulations, having her girlfriends
ager to know all about how she'd finally suc-
umbed to love and marriage…

She felt her throat close, painful and tight.
low could she have come to do what she had

done? Let herself fall in love with him again? When this time around she *knew* what kind of man he was! How could she have let her stupid, stupid heart betray her as it had?

And yet it had.

And it was agony to know it.

Nikos stood in Arrivals at Eleftheriou, tension in every muscle of his body. Calanthe's flight from Berlin had landed. She would be deplaning now. He knew she was returning to Athens because her father's housekeeper had mentioned it when he'd put in his daily call to Georgios, reporting back on his company's affairs.

Calanthe herself had not informed him. She had kept ruthlessly silent since leaving for London.

Her absence had given him the essential time he'd needed...

His muscles tensed again. So much depended on this.

Everything—my whole life...

But he would not—must not—let that show. He must stay...detached.

He craned his neck as another bevy of arriving passengers issued through from Customs. And there she was—walking swiftly forward, wearing a smart business suit in dark blue, low-heeled shoes, pulling a wheeled carry-on suitcase.

He stepped forward and he saw her face whiten with shock. He took her arm with one hand, relieved her of her carry-on with the other. She had stiffened at his touch, but he ignored it.

'How was your flight?' he asked her.

He kept his tone even, neutral, and she answered in kind.

'Fine,' she said.

She made to pull away, but he kept his hand on her forearm. It was as tense as steel.

'Good,' he said. 'Well, there's another one ahead of you.'

He started to guide her forward, but she balked.

'What do you mean?'

He paused, looking down at her. 'I mean,' he said, still keeping his voice neutral, 'we are going on our honeymoon.'

He saw her face whiten even more.

He cut across the protest rising on her lips. 'I have things to say to you, and they cannot be said in Athens.'

Rebuff flashed in her eyes. 'I don't want to hear them!'

'Tough,' he said.

He was in no mood to give any quarter. He'd steeled himself for this and he would see it through. He *must*.

He took a swift, incisive breath. 'You're going

to hear them even if I have to shout them ou
loud to you in the middle of this airport, for al
the world to hear! But the best place to hear then
requires a flight—a short one—by helicopter.'

She was resistant still. That was obvious. And
it was obvious why. He didn't care.

'Well?' he demanded. 'Are you going t
agree? Or do we stand here arguing in the mid
dle of Arrivals?'

Her face was set, but she made no more ver
bal resistance.

'Good,' he said again. 'The heliport is thi
way.'

He guided her forward, still in possession o
her carry-on. His touch was light, but insisten

Essential.

Just like the destination they were heading t

Calanthe strained away from Nikos in the clos
confines of the helicopter now speeding its wa
across the Aegean. Where they were heading
she neither knew nor cared. A profound wear
ness was washing over her and it was not just t
do with the flight from Berlin that morning.
was a weariness of the spirit that went so dee
inside her it was part of her very being.

It had been a part of her for a long, long tim
For eight long years.

Dully, she gazed out of the window. An islan

group was nearing, and the helicopter started to dip down towards one of the islands. It touched down on a characteristic large H, with nothing much around it except a marina. It looked gleaming and new, with the Greek flag flying jauntily from the harbourmaster's office and expensive motor yachts bobbing at their moorings, as well as some sailing craft.

A sudden fear struck her—please don't let Nikos be thinking of taking her on a yacht! In such tiny confines, with a crew all around them...or, worse, no crew at all, just her and Nikos...

As she jumped down from the helicopter after him, ignoring his outstretched hand, he led the way to a waiting taxi. She got in as Nikos stashed her carry-on and his own grip bag in the boot. As the taxi drove off she shut her eyes, glad that Nikos made no attempt to talk to her. But she had to open them perforce, a short while later, when the taxi drew to a halt outside what was clearly a resort hotel.

Though attractively designed—only two storeys high and set in landscaped grounds, with the sea just visible beyond—it did not look particularly upmarket, but more for general tourist visitors. Not something Nikos would choose at all.

She went inside, where the entrance gave

way to a large, airy atrium—again, attractively styled, but in no way at the level of a luxury hotel.

She turned back to Nikos, who was coming in after her with the luggage. 'Where is this?' she asked.

He paused. Looked at her. His gaze was veiled. 'Don't you recognise it?'

She looked at him blankly and shook her head.

'Ah, well,' he said, 'no reason you should. The last time you saw it, it was a building site.'

For a moment what he'd said made no sense. Then realisation flooded in. She gave a gasp. Of what, she wasn't quite sure.

He gave another nod as it dawned on her. 'Yes,' he said dryly, 'one and the same.' He glanced around him. 'Strange to think some of this is here due to my efforts. The foundations, mostly, and maybe part of the first storey.'

She was feeling faint. Faint with shock. It was washing over her in great waves.

What was she *doing* here? Why had she just numbly let Nik bring her here? And why did he want to be here?

Cold iced through her.

Please, please don't let him think he can recreate our time here eight years ago—pretend that what he did to me never happened...

He was speaking again, still in that same everyday tone of voice, as if her presence here was completely normal.

'I'll check us in. I've reserved a villa near the pool. Two bedrooms.'

She felt a fraction of the cold that had iced through her dissipate.

She glanced out of the tinted plate glass windows that looked out over gardens in which was set a massive pool—thronged, she could see, with children. On the far side, to the right, beyond more gardens, she could see tennis courts. She knew that underneath was the excavated archaeological site.

Time telescoped…past and present. She could almost see them all…students in two long rows, hunched over on their kneelers, flat pointed trowels teasing away the dry earth and stones, carefully, assiduously, patiently trying to reveal the past of three thousand years ago…

Eight years was nothing in that timeframe. The blink of an eyelid. But so, so long ago to her…

'Calanthe?'

Nikos's voice brought her back to the present. The present she did not want and could not avoid. Could not escape. He had a folder with their keys in it and was holding open the wide doors leading out to the gardens and the pool area. She walked forward, feeling the heat slam into her as they lost the air-con of the atrium.

She followed Nikos along a wide paved path, lined with bougainvillea, hibiscus and olean-der, all attractively planted, with stone benches and ironwork chairs and tables set along it, and parasols against the sun. They skirted the pool widely, heading, she realised, for a semicircle of little stone villas curving away from the pool area, overlooking the sea.

Each semi-detached villa was attractively built, with a balcony fronting the upper storey and a private terrace created in front at ground level, and hedging between the villas for privacy. As they passed one she heard gleeful laughter coming out, and children's cries in English.

'Come on, Dad! Let's get to the pool! I can't wait!'

She smiled in spite of herself. Children on hol-iday, families on holiday...far from soggy Eng-land which was having a wet summer.

'This is ours,' Nikos said, as they approached the end villa.

He set their baggage down at the wooden front door, painted Greek blue, just like the shutters and window frames, and opened the door, heft-ing up the luggage again.

There was something in the way his body moved that lanced memory through her. How eas-

y, eight years ago, his muscled body had tackled
ll that heavy lifting at the building site, as if what
e was carrying was papier-mâché. She shook the
nought from her…told herself instead that it was
wonder that a man as rich as Nikos was should
ower himself to carry his own luggage.

He gestured for her to go in and she did so.
mmediately cool air enveloped her, and she
vas glad. They were in a sitting/dining room
nat occupied the whole ground floor, with an
pen-plan kitchenette at the rear and a staircase
gainst the left-hand wall. It was attractively fur-
ished in blue and white—but, again, it was just
n ordinary family resort.

It was homely. Comfortable. Appealing.

Against her volition she liked it.

'Do you want to choose your bedroom?' Nikos
aid, poised at the foot of the wooden staircase.

She nodded briefly, following him upstairs.
he room at the front was larger—a double with
balcony—but she chose the smaller one at the
ack, a twin. Nik was welcome to the double
ed. Welcome to its solitary vastness.

She relieved him of her suitcase, closed the door
n him. Went and sat down on one of the beds.

She was feeling entirely blank.

ikos stepped out onto the balcony that opened
f his bedroom. There was a partial sea view,

and if he craned his head he could see part of the huge central swimming pool, but not the main resort building to the rear. It was strange to be back here—though 'strange' was an understatement…

Eight years ago he'd been a labourer here, turning a dirt field into a hotel.

Now he was staying here.

With his bride.

The word rang like a hollow, mocking joke, and he shifted restlessly. Had he been mad to bring Calanthe here? Yet somehow this place had seemed…appropriate.

It's where I first set eyes on her.

He felt the tension that racked him tighten unbearably. This place might also prove to be the last place he would ever set eyes on her.

Unless…

Tomorrow—tomorrow I will find out what my fate is to be.

He pulled his thoughts away. There was this evening to get through first.

CHAPTER TEN

'THERE ARE TWO restaurants here. The main one in the hotel, and then a more informal bistro-type near the pool.'

Nikos looked at her impassively and Calanthe tried to react similarly. But it was hard. Far harder than she wanted it to be.

To be here, in his company was hard, when the last time she had seen him it had been to hurl at him all those bitter, savage accusations that had eaten at her for all those years.

But not only was it hard for that reason. But for the very opposite.

Her gaze, still as impassive as she could make it, rested on him as they stood in the sitting room of the little villa. His presence was making itself felt on her consciousness...her senses. He was casually dressed, in chinos and an open-necked shirt, deck shoes and turned-back cuffs. Casual—devastating.

Irresistible.

The word he'd used about her now hovered i
her head about him. Memory added to it. Th
clothes he was wearing now were way more ex
pensive than those he'd worn when they'd gon
out in the evenings eight years ago, but he wor
them to the same effect. Her helpless gaze ha
clung to him then. It clung to him now.

'Or,' he was saying, as she tried to veil he
treacherous—irrelevant—reaction to him, 'w
could stay in. The restaurant has a delivery se
vice that we could use if you wish.' He pause
'Your call,' he said.

In her head, Calanthe heard the words *Non*
of the above! But for reasons she did not want t
admit to. Because she didn't want to have dinne
with Nikos at all. It would be just too...

Dangerous. That's what it would be.

Dangerous to spend any time with him at al
Dangerous to be with him. To gaze at him. Dar
gerous to be exposed to him...as if he carried a
infection she knew she would be unresistant t

What if he—?

She broke off her thought. What Nikos migl
try and do now that he had her to himself agai
was not to be given space inside her head.

'The poolside bistro,' she heard herself say.

That seemed the least bad option. Eating her
with him, was out of the question. And dining
the main restaurant, conscious of eyes all ov

the place, was not what she wanted either. So maybe the smaller bistro was preferable? Less showy?

More intimate?

No! Don't think of that. This was a family hotel, not a place for romantic couples. Surely that must reassure her?

He nodded. 'Bistro it is, then,' he said.

He crossed to the door, holding it open for her. She walked past him, burningly conscious suddenly of what she was wearing. Her suitcase contained only clothes appropriate for a conference, not a holiday resort. So she'd been glad to discover from the hotel guide left in the villa that there was a beach shop off the central atrium.

She'd waited until she'd heard Nikos leave the villa—he'd called out, in a deceptively casual tone, that he was going to catch a swim—and then warily made her way up to the hotel. She'd had to walk past the huge oval pool that dominated the gardens. There had still been some people in it, although not many at that late hour of the afternoon, but the only one she'd had eyes for was the swimmer who had been steadily ploughing the long length of it with a rhythmic, powerful freestyle.

Her breath had caught. His scything arms had sent up showers of water that caught the light of the lowering sun, creating a halo around his head, turning alternately left and right to draw breath as he swam. His powerful legs had threshed the water. She hadn't been able to see his body beneath the water. Only his shoulders, the upper part of his back. Bare and sculpted.

And so, so familiar.

She'd wrenched her gaze away, hurried her footsteps. As she'd walked up the shallow steps that led up to the terrace in front of the hotel she'd glanced sideways, catching a glimpse of the fencing around the tennis courts in the distance. Beneath their black surface lay the excavated remains of the dig, its contours mapped, its layout recorded, contents salvaged, and its presence now protected by the layer of hard standing carefully covering it.

But it was still there, deep beneath.

The past was always present, however deeply buried by the years…

Emotion had plucked at her, seeking entrance, but she'd held it back. Not giving it entrance. Nikos had brought her here, to a place she would never have set foot in again, and she had come, unknowing until it had been too late. But that did not mean she would not do her desperate best to protect herself. However hopeless the prospect.

The beach shop off the atrium had been full of buckets and spades, snorkelling kits and swimsuits. But there had also been some beachwear, and she had made her selection. She was wearing it now—a light cotton sundress in blue, with an elasticated waist and shoulder line.

The trouble was, she realised with a shimmer of dismay, the sundress was far too much like the outfit she'd worn to wow Nikos all those years ago.

Had he spotted the resemblance? She did not know and would not let herself care. He knew now, after what she had hurled at him on that hideous farce of a wedding night, that what he had done to her had exploded, for ever, whatever arrogant ambitions he'd had to win her back.

As for herself… Oh, dear God—now she was to suffer all over again. Eight years ago she had loved Nik, not knowing the depths to which he would stoop. And now—now she didn't even have that comfort…

The knowledge tortured her. But she must endure it.

Emotions swirled within her, powerful and chaotic and unnameable, each and every one of them unbearable.

'It's along here,' she heard Nikos say as he guided them forward, back up towards the pool, glowing iridescently now with underwater lights. There were a few last swimmers splashing around in it before it closed for the night.

Nikos led the way in the other direction from

where the distant tennis courts lay, down a pathway that meandered and then opened into a clearing in which a kiosk-style building declared itself to be the bistro. An appetising smell wafted from it.

'It seems to specialise in pizzas,' Nikos said wryly. 'Do you mind?'

Calanthe shook her head and he pulled out a chair for her at one of the outdoor tables set on a spacious circular paved area edged by oleander and bougainvillea. It was prettily lit by the lights strung around and suspended from wooden poles where more fairy lights were wound. Most of the tables were occupied by families, and she could catch various languages—from Greek and Italian to English and German.

She glanced across at the other diners. Happy people, happy families, on happy holidays...

Did her expression change as she looked at them...wondering, with a stab she wished she did not feel, whether she would ever have that herself?

Will it ever be mine? A husband to love me as I love him, and children for us both to love and make happy childhoods for?

Her expression hardened, and there was anguish in her suddenly averted eyes. Well, it would never be with Nik.

That stab of anguish was like a dagger in her heart—her stupid heart, broken all over again.

'Looks like this is a popular place—it's nice to see holidaymakers enjoying themselves,' she heard Nikos remark as a smiling young waitress plopped laminated menus down in front of them, ready to take their drinks order.

'We do our best.' The waitress smiled. 'The season's ending now, but we've been full on all summer.'

Nikos smiled at her. 'That's good,' he said.

Calanthe could see the waitress revelling in the impact of Nikos's smile.

He made me feel beautiful—warmed me with his smile...beguiled me with his kisses... Until—

She cut off her thoughts. There was no point remembering now. She knew what he was. And he knew that she knew.

He was relaxing back in his chair, still smiling at the young woman. 'I'll take a slice of the credit, I think. I worked here years ago, when it was nothing but a building site!'

The waitress's eyes widened. 'You?' she said.

Like Calanthe, she'd seen at once that he was wearing expensive clothes, an expensive wristwatch, handmade deck shoes—not the kind of things belonging a man who'd ever hauled bricks on a construction site.

He gave a laugh. 'It was hard work—and hot!

But…' He nodded. 'Looks like we did a good job. And I'm glad the resort is doing well.'

He glanced across at Calanthe and she had a sudden fear that he might tell the waitress that she, too, had once worked here—on an excavation. But he simply asked her what she might like to drink. She opted for sparkling water, and Nikos ordered a beer. The waitress smiled, and Calanthe could see her eyes lingering on Nikos as she headed off. Eyes would always linger on him.

Just as they did eight years ago. Like Georgia gazed after him, and all the other girls too.

And herself, most fatally of all.

'So, what kind of pizza?' Nikos asked.

He sounded enthusiastic, and Calanthe wondered at it. Pizza was a universe away from the gourmet meals he could now enjoy.

She glanced at the colourful menu, designed, obviously, to appeal to parents and children.

'*Pizza al funghi,*' she said, and set down the menu.

'OK. I'm going for pepperoni, chorizo, peppers and double cheese,' Nikos replied.

'Very authentic,' Calanthe heard herself say, her tone ironic.

He gave a half-laugh. 'Well, pizzas have evolved since Naples.'

The waitress was returning, depositing

Calanthe's water bottle and Nikos's half-litre glass of lager, glistening golden and beading gently.

He thanked the waitress, gave her their pizza orders. Then added: 'And a carafe of red—whatever's local.' He smiled.

She headed off again, throwing yet another lingering glance at Nikos.

He lifted his beer glass. *'Yammas,'* he said, and took a draught.

Calanthe poured a glass of fizzing water for herself, which tasted thin and prickling in her mouth. She did not return his casual toast.

She looked away, deliberately, towards a family a little way off. The father had a beer, like Nikos, and the mother a glass of white wine, fizzy drinks for the two children. They looked primary school age, she thought, and were busy working on the colouring sheets provided for their entertainment while waiting for their pizzas to arrive. The children were bickering, but amicably, clearly content and enjoying their holiday, and their parents were chatting to each other. Relaxed, carefree—on holiday and happy. She saw the dad lean forward for a moment, gently brush the mum's cheek. There was a soft look in his eyes, returned in full by his wife.

Unaccountably, she felt tears prick at the backs of her eyes. Blinked them away.

She envied them.

The arrival of their pizzas was timely, and
their aroma mouth-watering. She busied herself
with the cutting wheel, slicing up the massive
thick-crusted pizza, and Nikos did likewise. The
waitress came back with a carafe of red wine and
two glasses, taking her time filling each—as if,
Calanthe thought, she wanted to maximise her
time spent close to such a devastatingly attractive man as Nikos.

He thanked her with another melting smile
and Calanthe saw the girl's expression take on
a smitten look.

The way I used to gaze at him.

Her expression hardened. Well, much good
had done her.

Defiantly, she picked up her knife and fork
and attacked a slice of pizza with venomous
vigour, dropping her gaze down to it, looking
away from Nikos. And the girl gazing so help-
lessly at him.

'Is there anything else?' the waitress asked
Nikos, clearly hoping there was.

But he simply smiled again, shaking his head.
'It's all perfect,' he said. 'Thank you.'

And she coloured on cue, finally taking her
leave.

Calanthe got stuck in to eating, realising, as
she did so, that she'd swapped from drinking

water to reaching for a wine glass. She hadn't intended to drink any alcohol, but it was good, robust wine, and it went excellently with the pizza.

Nikos, too, had finished his beer and started on the wine.

He tilted his head slightly. 'The wine hasn't changed in eight years,' he said. 'Rough, but good for all that.'

She didn't answer, only took another mouthful of the wine. Feeling its impact on her. Giving her courage. She set down her glass, looked straight across at him.

'You dragged me here, Nikos, to this place, because you said you had "things to say" to me. So, what are they?' she challenged.

Yet even as she challenged him she felt a weariness of spirit assail her. What was the point of any of this? She felt a familiar pain squeeze her heart. Eight long years ago Nik had broken it. Now it would be broken all over again. This time because of her own stupidity.

This time around I knew what he was—but I still let it happen...

Her throat tightened with a familiar choking. And what good did that do her? None. Just as the ocean of tears she'd wept for him so long ago had never done her any good.

Nikos was answering her. His voice tight. 'This is not the time. Tomorrow.'

She looked across at him. Felt that weariness encompass her, that heaviness dull her senses.

'Whatever,' she said, and gave an indifferent shrug.

Then went back to eating her pizza. Went back to listening to the happy chatter of families on holiday...happy couples, with happy children.

She reached for her wine glass again, drained it, picked up the carafe, refilled her glass, poured the rest of the carafe's contents into Nikos's glass, then set the empty carafe back on the wooden table.

'You used to do that,' Nikos said slowly, watching her. 'Tell me to finish it off...that you'd had enough. Then you'd gaze across at me and I'd see in your eyes what any man would give a fortune to see.'

'But you didn't give a fortune, did you, Nik?' she heard herself answer. 'That besotted gaze of mine *gained* you a fortune. Or, if not a fortune, then at least a hefty pay-out.' She paused. 'My father told me exactly how much you cost him. Told me you doubled what you'd first been offered to leave me.'

She emptied her voice of emotion, because the emotion that would have been in it otherwise would have been unendurable to feel again.

'He told me that though you drove a hard bargain, and took him for more than he'd intended to pay, it had been worth every cent. He paid you willingly whatever it took to keep me safe from you.'

His face had closed. As if a steel shutter had come down over it. She saw him reach for his refilled wine glass, drain it to the dregs. As if he needed it. His cheekbones were stark, his mouth like a whipped line, his eyes completely masked. As if he could not bear to let her see what was in them.

And for a second—just the barest, briefest second—she wanted to see. Because there had been a flash—just a flash—of *something*. An emotion revealed, then instantly gone.

It might have been guilt.

Or even shame.

If he'd been capable of either.

But it had been neither.

For that brief second she had seen what surely should not be there—surely *could* not be there. What made no sense being there.

Pain.

CHAPTER ELEVEN

NIKOS'S HANDS WERE grimly steering the hire car along the winding coast road—not towards the new marina, with its heliport for the yacht owners, but to the island's main town, where the ferry port was.

The little harbour town along the coast from the resort and the former excavation site was not large enough for anything other than fishing craft and the vessels that had once plied their mercantile trade three thousand years ago across the eastern Mediterranean, leaving behind, millennia later, only the bare outline of their dwellings and warehouses, their bronze and ceramic household goods, their great amphorae that had once carried olive oil and wine, the cargo of the times.

His thoughts went to the resort hotel he'd taken Calanthe to—the one that he'd helped build with his bare hands. One day, in millennia to come, would the archaeologists of the future

e excavating the site? Unearthing remnants of
he people who had once been there? Not trad-
rs any longer, but holidaymakers. Every life a
ale to tell...

A tale long lost.

How hard it was to tell a tale that was lost.

How easy it was for tales to be lost.

To sink away into the past. Even the recent
ast. A mere eight years—an eye-blink—sep-
rated him and the woman now sitting silent,
withdrawn and hostile beside him and the man
nd woman they had once been.

But tales that could not be told—that had not
et been told—could fester and corrupt.

Eight years of festering and corruption...

'Are you going to tell me where you're tak-
ng me?'

Calanthe's cold voice pierced his circling,
rooding thoughts.

'As we get there,' was all he would say.

She fell silent again, simply gazing out of the
indow. The road was vaguely familiar to him.
Was it to Calanthe? She'd have left the island
his way, heading to the ferry port as they were
oing now.

He joined the queue and they drove slowly
hrough the town into the bowels of the waiting
erry. It was only a short crossing to the next is-
nd in the chain, hardly worth getting out of the

car. He said as much to Calanthe, but she undid her seat belt.

'Too claustrophobic,' she said, and got out, heading for the deck.

He did not follow her. Instead, he sat back, head against the headrest, gazing at nothing.

She came back just as the ferry docked at its destination, getting into the hire car and doing up her seat belt.

'Why have we come to this island?' she asked, as the hold doors slid slowly open and the cars started to emerge on to the quayside.

'To show you something,' was all Nikos said.

They drove out through the ferry port—very similar to the one they'd left, but larger, for this whole island was larger, if not by much. This island was familiar to him—long familiar.

Once again, he opted for the coast road, heading east. He did not look at Calanthe, but within a few kilometres of the town he saw her turn her head as they passed a road sign.

'*Aerodromio?*' she said. There was a clear question in her voice. 'Nikos, don't tell me we're *flying* somewhere now!'

'No,' he said.

He knew his voice was terse. But he was banking a lot down. And it was taking all his strength, his nerve, to keep it banked down. He felt his emotions stress and strain, like fractured plates in the earth's crust, rubbing and grinding against each other. The pressure building up, unable to be released.

As they approached the airport he didn't take the road that branched off to the entrance, nor did he keep to the main road that followed the coastline, a half-kilometre or so to their right. Instead, he slowed and took an unmarked dirt road leading off the left.

He knew exactly where it went.

It circled the northern perimeter fence, the high mesh that separated the airport area from the countryside around it.

He drove between the fence to his right and the olive groves that stretched to the left, hectare after hectare, spreading widely inland. A few houses were dotted around, and some stone sheds, but not many. The trees were heavy with olives—in a few weeks the harvest would begin. The whole area was extensive, marked off by old stone walls, many crumbling now, into holdings owned by any number of islanders.

When it was time for harvest, it was usually a communal affair. He remembered it well from his youth, with neighbours pitching in to help each other, all hands on, including his own hands, even when he was a small child.

The children always enjoyed themselves—it was almost like a party. Someone would bring a

football, and there would be a kick-around when
the adults were busy or had no tasks for them
Then someone would call them, and the children
who were old enough, but not too heavy, would
shin up the olive trees to help knock down any
recalcitrant fruit on to the waiting nets spread
out below to catch them.

'Where are we going?'

Calanthe's question recalled him to the pres
ent.

'We're nearly there,' he said.

He drove a little further, careful of the wheel
on the rutted track. Then, at a spot he knew wel
he stopped, cut the engine.

'I want to show you something,' he said.

He got out of the car, feeling those tectoni
plates inside him again, fractured and cracked
grinding against each other. Still seeking release

Soon, but not quite yet.

She got out as well, and in the silence the im
mediate chorus of cicadas was all about ther
as the mid-morning sun beat down. There wa
a tumbling stone wall less than a metre high t
their left, and he stepped through a gap, turnin
so that both the car and the airport's perimete
fence were in front of him.

Without him asking, Calanthe came and stoo
beside him. But she was not looking at the ai
port—rather at the olive trees all around.

'Looks like there'll be a good harvest,' she said, as if searching for something to say.

'Yes. I've given a hand here many a time… helping my grandmother.' He paused. 'She owned a good few hectares of olive trees.'

Calanthe glanced around her. 'Which were hers?' she asked.

He nodded towards the airport. 'Over there,' he said.

Calanthe frowned. 'Oh, that's a shame!' she exclaimed. 'But I guess maybe the island wanted an airport?'

'It did,' Nikos confirmed. 'It was controversial at the time—a dozen years ago or so—and I remember a lot of debate, with a lot of pros and cons thrashed out in the local newspapers and in the bars and tavernas. In the end, as you can see, it went ahead.' His voice changed a little. 'It's helped to encourage more tourism, and helped develop the island economically—reduce its dependence on farming and fishing.'

'Isn't that a good thing?'

Though there was a question in her voice, she knew it was not just about the subject under discussion. Why was it under discussion at all. What was going on?

'Overall, yes. Except that when there are projects like this, issues like this, there are always winners...' He paused. 'And losers.'

He walked away, along the line of the old tumbling wall, and Calanthe followed him, placing her footsteps carefully in the rough grass. Some way ahead of her, Nikos stopped again. She caught up with him and he nodded towards the section of airport behind a white two-storey building.

Beyond it was a single runway. As well as the cicadas all around, Calanthe started to hear the noise of a plane's engines, approaching from over the sea, its port and starboard lights blinking at the edges of its wings as it came into view, its descent quickening. It wasn't a large plane, just a standard tourist charter, easily capable of using the scale of runway here. It banked, and then landed with a deafening roar, engines in noisy retro thrust to slow its speed.

Calanthe put her hands over her ears until the engines cut out. 'Well, anyone living too close to that would definitely be one of the losers!' she exclaimed.

'Not that much,' Nikos said. 'Except in high season there aren't many flights. There were other losers, though.'

She looked at him. His voice had changed. Taken on an edge.

'And winners,' he went on, with the same edge

in his voice. He nodded to the building in front of them. 'Old Stavros was one of the winners. He was a shrewd old boy, and he owned as many hectares of olive trees as my grandmother. All of them are now under the other half of the airport, abutting my grandmother's land. Stavros liked to keep his ear to the ground...keep an eye on what people were doing. Including my grandmother,' he said, and now there was a heavy note in his voice. He paused. 'He played his cards very close to his chest, though. Few people got the better of him.'

Calanthe looked at him. There must be some point to this, but she had no idea what. Was Nikos about to tell her why he'd brought her here?

It seemed not.

He turned on his heel, his back towards her.

'Let's get back to the car,' he said.

There seemed to be tension in his voice now, and his face was set.

She frowned, but followed him, stepping through the gap in the wall and getting back into the car.

He turned it around, heading back the way they'd come. Once on the main road he drove back towards the ferry port and then, a few kilometres along, turned inland onto a metalled but narrow road, towards the island's hilly centre.

They drove through a small village with a little church, a single bar, a mini-supermarket and a pharmacy, and out the other side, all the time gaining height. Then, about a kilometre beyond the village, a stone wall extended to their right, with a wooden gate in it. Inset into the wall was a ceramic plaque declaring, in both Greek and Roman lettering, *Villa Irene*.

'Irene,' Nikos remarked, 'was the name of my grandmother.'

He drove slowly through the gate, between oleander bushes, and pulled up outside a solid-looking house with white-painted shutters and a white door. It looked neat and attractive, with large glazed ceramic pots either side of the front door, vivid with red geraniums.

'This is her house,' Nikos announced, cutting the car's engine.

He got out, and Calanthe did likewise. She was aware that her heartrate had quickened a little.

'It's very pretty,' she said, politely and truthfully.

'I grew up here,' Nikos said. 'It was just my grandmother and me. After she died—three years ago—I kept it. It needed doing up a bit... She always refused to modernise, even when she knew I could easily afford it. Nowadays I let it out—it's marketed as a "rustic retreat", for those wanting to get away from it all and experience what's left of authentic rural life.'

'It suits that perfectly.' Calanthe nodded appreciatively.

'A neighbour looks after it—sees to the garden, cleans inside and so on. There's no one staying at the moment, though.'

He stooped to retrieve a large, old-fashioned key from under one of the flowerpots, and opened the door. It was cool inside, because of the thick walls, and simply decorated, in keeping with the building's style. Calanthe could not help but like it.

How strange to think of Nikos as a young boy, growing up here.

She frowned. How had he come from being here—a local lad, helping out with the olive harvest, part of a village community with traditional values—to behaving as he had. Being paid off by a rich man...paid to desert his infatuated daughter...

Was the temptation too great for him to resist? He was putting himself through university...working on building sites during vacations. Then my father offered him so much money could he just not bring himself to refuse it?

And if that were so...her frown deepened... was that excuse enough?

She thought back to her own upbringing. OK,

she had always known that she had a rich father in the background—had experienced the luxury he enjoyed when she visited him during school holidays—but her mother had raised her with sound principles that befitted their modest circumstances.

What if our roles had been reversed? What if Nikos had been an infatuated young man and his rich father had thought me a scheming gold-digger...tried to pay me off?

Would she have taken the money?

She knew the answer. Knew it clear and confirmed. No, she would not. There were things decent people did, and things they didn't. What Nikos had done was one of them.

Her expression hardened.

He was heading into what was clearly the main room, with a fireplace set in one wall, flanked by comfortable-looking traditional-style seating, and with a wooden dining table and solid-looking chairs at the far side, next to a door going through to what she could see was the kitchen.

The whole room had a welcoming ambience, and she liked it instinctively. There was a large, handsome armoire against another wall—made out of olive wood, she guessed, and beautifully painted with ornamental flowers and scrolls in ultra-traditional style. An original piece, she reckoned, and felt drawn to it automatically.

'This is beautiful!' she exclaimed.

'Part of my grandmother's dowry when she married. It had been her grandmother's before. There is some similar painted furniture up-stairs—one of the old beds and another armoire, and some smaller pieces too.'

'How lovely that they're still here,' Calanthe could not help saying.

She looked around her. There were some paintings on the wall, in a rustic style. One showed an ancient ruin and a girl sitting in tra-ditional Greek costume from several hundred years ago. Another showed a large, handsome goat—presumably a prized animal from long ago. Yet another was a still-life, of a ceramic jug full of flowers.

She heard Nikos opening the armoire and turned. He was extracting a box file, and after closing the door he crossed the room to deposit it on the table. Calanthe watched him, half curi-ous, half frowning, conscious that her heartrate was still raised.

Wondering why, exactly.

Her eyes rested on Nikos. She tried to see him as he must once have been, growing up here, a strong lad, tall for his age—already showing, she

was sure, the devastating good-looks he would
have as a teenager.

Had he broken local hearts? she wondered.

As well as mine?

'I'd like to show you something.'

Nikos's words were a welcome interruption to
thoughts that were pointless to have. As pointless
as her thinking now, as she crossed to where he
stood, how good he looked in that open-necked
shirt, the same one he'd worn last night, the
cuffs not turned back this time, how his dark
hair feathered at the nape of his strong neck, how
his long eyelashes dipped over his dark eyes,
how his sculpted mouth brought back memories
she must not indulge...

Yet they pressed for ingress all the same.

So many, many memories...

An ache opened inside her, raw and intense.
Anguished was tearing at her. To see Nikos here
in the house he grew up in, to remember how
he'd been that golden summer of her youth, how
totally she'd fallen for him, how ardently she'd
given herself to him, wanting nothing more than
for that summer to go on and on...never to end.

Never—dear God—to end as it had.

*He took my father's money. Let himself be
paid off. Shameful and despicable.*

Her eyes were shadowed as she walked towards the table. Nikos had reappeared in he

life, out of the blue, and made clear that she had
once again aroused in him the same fire of desire that had flared before.

As had he, so fatally, in her, that night at the
beach hut.

*But I was strong then. At least afterwards—in
the morning. Strong enough to leave him.*

And to regret, bitterly, her weakness.

But not strong enough to stop herself doing
what she should never have allowed herself to
do again...

She felt her heart squeeze with pain.

'Calanthe—'

His voice penetrated the fog of her hopeless
thoughts. A wave of that familiar heavy weariness swept over her again. All this traipsing
around from island to island. A helicopter, a taxi,
a hire car, a ferry... An olive grove, an airport
and now his grandmother's old house.

What was it for?

What purpose could it serve?

*He is who he is. Venal and corrupt. There is
nothing more. I have to accept it.*

But she was here now, and she would see it
through.

He was lifting two documents out of the box
file. They had a formal, legal look to them, and
were both very similar.

She drew closer and he placed one of them in

front of her. It was a contract of sale. She glanced at it, frowning, not knowing what she was supposed to be seeing.

'I mentioned Stavros to you when we were down by the airport. I told you he was shrewd old guy...that few ever got the better of him. This contract shows it.'

He paused, pointing to where the legalese was interrupted by the typed identification of a specific piece of land.

'This is his olive grove. The one that is now under half of the airport.' He paused. Pointed at another typed-in line. 'This is the sum he received for it.'

Calanthe's eyebrows rose. It was an extremely large sum for just an olive grove. Except, of course, she realised, it was no longer an olive grove but part of a commercial airport.

Nikos was moving the document aside, replacing it with the other one. 'Take a look at this one,' he said.

It was identical to the first, except for two things—the identity of the plot of land and the sum paid for it. She frowned. Massively less than the first.

'The two plots were the same size,' Nikos was saying.

There was something strange about his voice. She looked at him, still frowning.

He lifted away the top page of each document, revealing the pages behind. Another couple of paragraphs of legalese, and then two sets of signatures. One was common to both—somebody from an outfit called Venture Land. The other was different on each.

One was Stavros's signature.

The other was Irene's—Nikos's grandmother.

'Look at the dates,' Nikos was saying now.

She did. His grandmother's contract was dated three months before Stavros's.

She looked up at Nikos, still not understanding. 'So?' she said.

His voice was hollow as he answered her. 'Agreement to build the new airport was made public a fortnight after my grandmother sold her olive grove to Venture Land. Had she waited a mere two weeks it would have been worth what Old Stavros got for his—way more than she received!'

Calanthe swallowed. 'That *is* wretched,' she allowed. 'But if no one knew whether the airport would get planning permission when she sold, then wasn't the buyer taking a risk buying her land at all? He might have ended up with just another olive grove.'

'Unlikely.' Nikos's voice was hard as iron.

He drew out another document—this time,

Calanthe could see, it was the printout of an email.

'You see, the date stamp on this email shows that the sender had received private information—a copy of a signed document from a key member of the planning committee saying that the airport was definitely getting the go-ahead. The vote had already been taken and, crucially, the exact site it would occupy confirmed. It was just a question of timing the announcement. The sender, therefore, had inside knowledge. As, therefore, did the recipient.' He thrust the email printout at her. 'Take a look at who that is.'

She saw the name—it meant nothing to her. But then she saw who the email had been copied to.

Her eyes flew to Nikos. Stricken. 'My *father*?'

Her voice was as stricken as her face.

'The very same.' There was a dark savagery in Nikos's voice.

She dropped the printout as if it were toxic. 'But…but… Venture Land…' She floundered, trying to make sense of it. 'I've never heard of it. What's it got to do with Petranakos?'

'It's a subsidiary. A small one—one of several. A major company such as Petranakos, Calanthe, can find it…useful sometimes not to declare an interest in a particular piece of land. After all,' he went on, with the same savagery in his voice,

f someone turned up at your door to buy a per-
ctly ordinary olive grove and they were from
etranakos Property... Well, even the simplest
erson might wonder what their interest was.
ut if it was just a small company called Venture
and, operating in just these few islands, who
id they had an interest in working with olive
l producers—nothing large-scale, just adding
their holdings here and there as plots became
ailable... My grandmother had already made
ear in the village that hers was for sale—why
ould she think anything of it? She was offered
fair price for an olive grove of that size, num-
r of trees and general yield. Why would she
fuse?'

His voice changed. 'You see,' he said, 'she
anted to make it easier for me to pursue my
udies. Architecture is a long course, and she
ew it would take me a long time to qualify.'

'She sold the grove to help you,' Calanthe said.
She could feel her stomach churning, things
arranging themselves in her head. Things she
d not want to be rearranged.

'Yes. I didn't want her to, but she was ad-
nant. She was so proud that I'd got on the
urse—a village boy, on a top architectural
urse! I was already at university when she
ent ahead with the sale.'

Calanthe saw his fists clench.

'She did it without telling me. Without warning me. If I'd known—' He broke off.

Something in his eyes made Calanthe blench.

'She was a simple, decent woman. An honourable woman. Selling part of her inheritance for my sake... Selling it, so she thought, for a fair price, to a fair buyer... And all along—' He thrust the contract of sale for Stavros's holding at her. '*This* was the fair price of her land! *This* was what Stavros held out for! He saw how much my grandmother got and sat tight. Refused to part with his land.' He inhaled sharply. 'He didn't sell until the announcement was made confirming the airport would be built and the site. Then the price of his land rocketed. And Stavros got the true market value.'

He sat down abruptly, yanking the box file closed, replacing everything he'd taken out of it. Then he looked at Calanthe.

'I find it ironic,' he said, 'that it is only because I now have access to all the Petranakos business records that I can present you with the evidence I needed to show you. Oh, I've got my grandmother's paperwork for this and all her other affairs, such as they were, in a safety deposit box in the local bank here. But without proof that Venture Land is part of Petranakos—without their copy of the contract of sale for Stavros's holding and without the email trail showing that Venture Land and Petranakos had insider knowledge about the airport—you would just have dismissed all this.'

He paused, laying his hands flat on the closed box file.

'Perhaps there is one other thing that it may be…helpful…for you to know.'

He rested his eyes on her as she stood there, stomach still churning, thoughts in chaos, dismay roiling within her. His gaze was dark and cold, and it cut her like a knife.

'My grandmother sold her olive grove for the sum you saw on her contract. Stavros sold his for the sum on his. Take one from the other. What number comes up? You do the maths.'

He paused—a deadly pause.

'Does that precise amount sound familiar to you?'

She shut her eyes. There was a drumming in her ears.

'It's what my father paid you,' she said.

Her voice seemed to come from a very long way away.

Nikos smiled. 'Got it in one,' he said.

CHAPTER TWELVE

So HE HAD told her. Told her just why, eight year
ago, when Georgios Petranakos had sent his fix
ers in to put it to him that he might like to con
sider the offer they were willing to make him
he had not sent them packing.

Now, eight years later, he pushed aside th
box file, looked up at Calanthe. 'You'd better s
down,' he said. 'I don't want you passing out c
me, and you've gone white as a sheet.'

He watched her numbly collapse down on or
of his grandmother's dining chairs. She put h
hands on the table, holding them tightly togethe
so the knuckles showed as white as her face.

'You were just evening the score,' she sai
and he could see what each word was costin
her.

'Yes,' said. 'I was just evening the score. Yo
father's fixers weren't happy—they wanted n
to accept the sum they'd offered me. But I he
out. It was peanuts for your father—I knew th

and they knew that—but they were careful with his money all the same. For me, the sum I got out of them was simply...justice.'

He sat back, ran a hand through his hair. Tiredness filled him, and a sense not of vindication but simply of resignation.

'Does it make any difference to you?' he asked.

His voice was tired. He was tired of all this. Tired because he suspected none of it was of any use. Not even what he now asked her.

'Does it make any difference to you, Calanthe, if I say the rest of it? That your father's fixers needn't have bothered to offer me anything at all.' His eyes rested on her. 'Because they could have achieved their ends without costing your father a cent.'

He frowned, fingering the edge of the box file, looking down at the surface of the table where he had eaten all his meals as a child, so familiar that if he listened hard enough he could almost hear his grandmother moving around in the kitchen, putting pots and pans away, not letting him help, telling him he must get on with his homework instead.

'Studying is important, Nikki—with education, the world is yours!'

He had believed her—and it was true. The world was his. He had achieved so much—for himself, certainly, and even something for the world as well. Safer housing and offices and factories for those threatened by earthquakes.

His eyes lifted to the woman sitting opposite him. So beautiful, even with her face so pale, her eyes so stricken. She had caught his eye from the very first, but she had not liked his attention… had resisted him at first.

But he'd won her round. Won her, full stop. Made her his. And to him she'd entrusted her virginity—a gift he'd cherished. Honoured.

What did I feel for her then, all those years ago?

Even now he was not sure.

But of one thing he *was* sure, and he would tell her so.

He drew a breath, spoke again. 'Your father didn't need to pay me off.' He met her eyes. 'You see, the moment I realised who you were I knew I had to end it.'

He saw her eyes widen. Saw her not understanding.

He took another breath. 'Calanthe, there's a name for poor men who make up to the daughters of rich men. It's not a name I ever wanted. And had your father been *any* rich man other than the man he was his fixers would have got short shrift from me! But all the same I'd have done what they wanted. Finished with you and left you. But instead…' his eyes would not let hers drop '…because of who he was, and because of what he'd done to my grandmother, I took his money—everything that I held out for. And then I left you. Left you to go back to my grandmother. To give her the cheque they'd given me, made out to her, not me.'

His voice changed, tightened. There was bitterness in it now.

'So your father has never known that I am the man he paid off all those years ago. My grandmother took the cheque because I told her that I'd confronted the head honcho of the company that had bought her olive grove and demanded from them its true value—and got it.'

She spoke finally, her voice low and stricken. 'I've always thought my father an honourable man who made his money fairly—' She broke off.

'Maybe he did—mostly,' Nikos said. 'For all I know, in this particular instance, his Venture Land front man simply tried it on and got away with it. Maybe that email I showed you with your father's name on it was never read by him. Maybe it was just filed by his PA along with hundreds of others. My grandmother's olive grove was small fry…even the airport was small fry—just one of scores of other land deals your father has struck in his time through the people he employs and the subsidiaries he's set up.'

She looked at him, anguish in her eyes. 'Or maybe you might just be...be trying to make it easier for me.'

'Maybe I am,' he said, his voice weary. 'But does it? If it counts at all, the reason I told your father's men that you must never know was that I didn't want you hurt. But your father...' He sighed. 'Your father thought it best you were hurt. To protect you from the man he thought I was.'

And am I that man, after all?

Tiredness washed over him again. He had staked everything on this moment, on trying to justify what he'd done. And now—

Abruptly, she pushed back her chair. It scraped on the stone floor. 'I need... I need...'

She didn't finish. Only walked rapidly from the room. He heard the front door open, and then silence.

He picked up the box file, replaced it in the painted armoire that had been there all his life, as solid and sound as the house he'd grown up in, as the grandmother who'd raised him.

He followed Calanthe out into the garden. She was standing with her back to him, arms folded defensively, her shoulders hunched. He came up behind her, but not too close.

Keeping his distance.

That was essential.

'I don't know whether I did right or wrong n taking your father's money as I did,' he said lowly. 'But this I do know. I never regretted it. regret a lot—but not that.'

She turned, her arms still tightly folded as if o protect herself, keep him at bay. 'Do you regret things, Nikos? What do you regret?'

Her voice was low. Sunlight was playing on er hair. Gilding the honey of her skin. How eautiful she was—how breathtakingly, wonrously beautiful...

As she had always been.

From the very first to the very last.

As this, surely, was the last.

'I regret having to leave you that golden sumertime,' he said. 'I've told myself I would have ft you anyway, even had I never known whose aughter you were, because you were just a sumer romance. You were so young, and I had to ake my way in the world. I had nothing to offer ou then. Yet for all that I would still have left ou with regret. Wishing I did not have to. Wishg...' He took a breath, ready to say now, all ese years later, what he had told himself was t so. 'Wishing I could ask you to wait for me.'

It was said—what he had barely given head ace for.

He had told himself that what they had was only a summer romance, that it could not last, could never be more than that.

And when I discovered who she was I had to cling to that fiction.

Her eyes were on him, her folded arms still keeping him at bay. Still protecting herself, as if stanching a wound. Then she spoke, her voice low and anguished.

'I would have waited, Nikos. Because I was in love with you.'

Her eyes were pained, and no longer because of what he'd told her at his grandmother's dining table. He could see there were other reasons now. Reasons beyond that.

'I was in love with you, and it broke my heart when you left me. And I would have gone on yearning for you…hoping and hopeless…wanting you back. So my father told me what you'd done.' Her voice hollowed. 'So that I could stop loving you—and hate you instead.'

She looked away for a moment, then back at him.

'But I have no cause to hate you, Nik. Not now.'

She looked around her and he saw her expression—so drawn and stark and stricken—soften a fraction.

'I shall think of you here, Nikos. That will

be good, I think. Because this is a good house, and your grandmother was a good woman, and she raised you, as I now know, to be a good man. I've wasted years hating you. Now at least I can let that go. What a waste it all was,' she said sadly.

He saw her dip her head, saw the sun burnishing her hair, setting a halo around it. Saw, too, slow tears oozing down her cheeks.

He felt himself step forward. Reach out his hand. Touch her lowered cheek with his outstretched finger.

'Don't weep,' he said. His voice was low. 'Don't weep for the waste of it. I was never worth it. But you...you, Calanthe, have always been worth it—always! In that golden summer *and* now. Above all now.'

He let his hand fall away, felt his fingertip wet with her slow tears.

'Eight years ago it did not matter what I felt for you. You were Georgios Petranakos's daughter and you were beyond me. And my duty...' he drew a heavy breath '...my duty was to my grandmother, to ensure she was no longer cheated of what was her due. Then, when I saw you again in Athens, at your father's side, even more beautiful than you had ever been, I knew that all I had wanted that summer long ago was what I wanted again. You in my arms again. In my bed. And

when your father needed me…then it all seeme
so perfect for me. Until—'

He broke off. Then he made himself say wh
he must.

'Before, it was you who loved me and I wh
turned my back on you. Now, all these year
later, it is you who has turned your back on me

He paused, frowning. Looking away from he
Not able to bear to look at her.

'I thought,' he said, and he heard a bleaknes
in his own voice that tore him in pieces, 'that i
marrying you I was getting everything I wante
But…' his voice was ragged now '…in fact I wa
losing it all.'

He made himself look at her, meet her strick
eyes with his.

'Losing you, Calanthe, the woman that th
time I knew with all my heart I had come
love.'

He heard a cry break from her. Break fro
her heart broken so long ago as his was new
broken. Tears were pouring down her face. Tea
he could not bear to see. Tears he must wi
away. Kiss away.

She came into his arms. Clinging to him w
broken sobs. His hands framed her face, his fi
gers clutching at her, and he was bending to k
her eyes urgently, desperately.

'Do you mean it, Nikos?' Her voice was a whisper…a plea.

'With all my being,' he told her, and his voice was rich with emotion. 'At first I thought that all I felt was desire,' he said, and his voice was different now, stronger and full of wonder. 'A desire I could now fulfil, for I belonged to your world… had earned my place in it. But then…' He took a breath, ragged and raw. 'It took your denunciation of me on our wedding night, your rejection of me, to show me the truth of what I felt for you! Desire, yes—oh, yes, always and for ever! But also—oh, my most adored Calanthe—so, so much more.'

His name broke from her and he swept her to him. Emotion was rising in him like a tsunami, and he held her tightly, fiercely, against him.

She was gazing up at him, and what he saw in her eyes made him reel.

'I never stopped loving you,' she said. 'I tried… I tried and failed. Whatever my father told me…whatever I told myself. Even though I knew and believed that what you had done was torture to me—still I went on loving you. Though I buried it as deep as it was possible to do. Until—'

She broke off. Spoke again.

'When you came back into my life—oh, dear God—I felt it all start again. Hating you and loving you. And I could not bear it! But now…'

There was something new in her voice, like a bird breaking free of a cage after beating its wings in vain.

'Oh, Nik, my dearest, darling one, now I need only love you.'

The joy in her voice turned his heart over. He kissed her slowly, gently, his senses still reeling, and she kissed him back. Softly, lovingly...

'What happens now, Nikos?' she asked, her voice low, as she drew back from him a little.

'Will you stay with me?' he asked, his voice just as low. 'Will you stay with me, my bride, my wife...my love?'

She gazed up at him, her eyes shining like stars. 'Oh, yes,' she breathed. 'Oh, *yes*.'

It was the answer he craved. The only answer he could bear to hear. Now and for ever. It took him to heaven on wings of gold. And he was flying there with her.

'This,' Calanthe declared, 'is the best pizza ever—it's official!'

'It's the same one you ordered last night,' Nikos pointed out, lifting a slice of his own—also exactly the same as he'd ordered the night before.

'It's completely different!' she riposted. 'Be-cause...' she reached a hand across the wooden table at the poolside bistro, her other hand precariously holding a slice of fully loaded *pizza al funghi*, threads of melted mozzarella trailing '... *I* am completely different!'

She shut her eyes. Could happiness such as this truly be real? It radiated from her like sunshine, brighter than anything she had ever known. Filled her from within. Every cell in her body...every fibre of her being.

She gazed across the table at him as he took a mouthful of his own pizza, cocking a quizzical eyebrow at her as he did so. He was smiling, his eyes alight with a warmth that took her breath away. Not letting her gaze drop for even a second, an instant, she bit into her own pizza slice.

At the table next to theirs was seated the same family as last night, the two children filling in their colouring sheets, their parents smiling at each other with fondness, secure in their love for each other.

Calanthe felt her heart squeeze.

Last night she had thought such happiness could never be hers—and now it was. Hers for ever.

It swept over her, wave after wave, as she steadily demolished the pizza, washing it down with the robust local red wine. Nikos did likewise. What they talked about she hardly knew... except that conversation came as easily now as it once had all those years ago.

'How long can we stay here? At the resort?' she asked him as, replete with pizza, she finally pushed the denuded wooden platter aside, reaching for her wine glass and leaning back comfortably in her chair.

'As long as we like,' Nikos answered. He refilled his glass, then realised that he'd drained the carafe. 'Shall we order more wine?' he asked.

She shook her head. 'You finish it,' she said. She frowned. 'But what about work?'

'What about it?' he returned easily. He leant forward. 'It can wait—both your father's company and my own. Because this, my adored Calanthe, is our honeymoon.' His voice was husky as he looked around him. 'Mind you, I had envisaged somewhere more glamorous, I must say. I was planning for the Seychelles, the Maldives...the South Seas, even.'

She waved away such possibilities. They were unnecessary and irrelevant.

'Here,' she said, 'is perfect.'

She looked around. It *was* perfect. Perfect because it was a happy place, for happy families having a happy holiday. Perfect because she was here with Nikos and he was all she needed and would ever need to be happy.

She felt her heart turn over. She gazed at him, her eyes filled with lovelight. All that she had nce dreamed of…yearned for…longed for… as now hers.

She finished her wine, setting her glass back n the table. She saw the young waitress bringg the family next to them their pizzas, heard e happy exclamations of the children, their couring sheets set swiftly aside.

She and Nikos had dined early—and she knew hy. She watched as Nikos finished off his own ine, then looked across at her. He said not a ord—only got to his feet. She did likewise. She aited while he reached into his pocket, drew t his wallet, put down a generous tip for the ung waitress, slipping it under his wooden atter, then repocketed his wallet.

He held out his hand to Calanthe and she took folding her fingers into his warm, strong hand. They walked away down the dim path, nightented with honeysuckle, the cicadas serenadg them as they headed back to their little villa. hey stepped inside, still hand in hand, wordss and unhurried, for neither words nor haste ere necessary now.

At the top of the stairs Nikos turned to her d said simply, 'My bed is larger.'

She gave a laugh, low and happy. 'Perfect,' e said.

And it was.

Quite, quite perfect.

* * *

She was velvet in his arms. Velvet and silk and satin. And her mouth was honey and peach. Anything and everything that was sweet and wonderful and wondrous.

With languorous kisses and leisurely caresses he roused her to all that she desired, receiving back from her, with her gliding hands and sweetest lips, all that he could ever desire for himself. Until, holding back no longer, he claimed her in his burning desire and found something he had never known before.

His newfound love for her consumed him, consumed them both. And as their moment of union came…as their bodies fused into one glorious, transcendent whole, possessed by ecstasy…he heard her cry out, sobbing even as it broke through him like a tumultuous wave. He threw back his head to echo her cry, deeper and louder, as her body convulsed around him and her arms clung to him, her thighs wrapping round his to hold him to her, never to let him go, rocking him in the cradle of her hips as her body shuddered beneath his.

And as she quietened, tremor after tremor still quivering through her, he smoothed her tumbled hair with a shaky hand, every muscle in his body slackening. His heart was still thundering, and hers was beating against his, and he drew her with him as he slipped from her, letting his head rest on the pillow beside her, lifting a hand to trace, with wondering gentleness, the contours of her parted lips.

He gazed into her eyes, knew there was wonder in his as in hers.

'I never knew...' he said. 'I never knew the difference love makes.'

She gave a choke, a smothered cry, burying her face in his chest and wrapping her arms around him more tightly yet.

He stroked her hair softly and tenderly, felt wonder and gratitude filling him. And love... such love...possessing him...

Slowly, driftingly, as they were held in each other's arms, sleep finally took them.

And love held them close for ever.

EPILOGUE

'MY DEAREST, DEAREST DAUGHTER…' Georgios P
tranakos's voice was warm, and rich with emo
tion. His glance went to Nikos. 'And you, whos
love for her will always keep her safe!'

He was lifting a glass of vintage champagn
tilting it towards them both. He was lookin
well, his recovery from major surgery definite
underway. True, he wasn't supposed to be drin
ing alcohol for a good while yet, but Calanth
hadn't the heart to stop him on this particul
day.

Her wedding day.

Her *second* wedding day.

Her *proper* wedding day, as both her fath
and her husband called it.

And she did too.

She lifted her own glass to Nikos now, and
did the same to her.

'My adored bride,' Nikos said softly, lovelig
in his eyes.

'My darling husband,' she murmured in return, her eyes shining with love and happiness.

Their church wedding earlier that day had been a quiet affair—both she and Nikos had insisted on it. They did not want to risk any over-exertion by her father. Later, when he was stronger still, they would hold a lavish wedding party, invite all of Athens, but for now what both she and Nikos truly valued was having made their vows to each other—vows of love and matrimony that could never be broken.

Love filled her. So much love for her beloved Nikos. Hers now for ever and ever!

It was a love that her father understood—endorsed. They had told him everything—all that had estranged them. He had found it hard to accept that Nikos was, indeed, the same young man he had wanted to protect her from all those years ago, but when they'd told him just why he had accepted Georgios's money it had been her father's turn to be abashed. To Calanthe's intense relief, the explanation that Nikos had ventured—that perhaps Georgios himself had not known of how Nikos's grandmother had been underpaid so shamefully—had been confirmed by her father.

'My boy, believe me from my heart,' he'd said to Nikos, taking his hand. 'Never, *never* would I have knowingly cheated anyone of a fair price for their land! The man who did so no longer works for me.'

It had been all that she and Nikos needed to hear. Now only a golden future in endless love and happiness awaited them.

And one more joy.

As her father toasted them both again, wreathed in beaming smiles, she took another sip from her champagne flute. But only a small one.

'You are not the only one who must abstain from alcohol for a while, Papa,' she said, lowering her glass. 'You see…'

She turned to Nikos, and a secret smile passed between them.

'Shall we?' she murmured.

He took a mouthful of his champagne. 'Most certainly,' he assured her, his eyes entwining with hers.

She took a breath…looked at her expectant father.

'You must get as well as you can, Papa, as fast as you can,' she told him. 'Because Nikos and I want you to be as active and vigorous a grandfather as your forthcoming grandchild will need… In fact, we insist!'

A shout of delight broke from Georgios and he enveloped Calanthe in a bear hug that made her catch her breath. Then he was seizing Nik's hand and pumping it excitedly.

He stood back. 'You have given me the greatest happiness,' he said, addressing them both. His eyes went from one to the other, reading each of them, 'And you will give each other the greatest happiness too.'

He gave a sigh of satisfaction, looked again at his daughter.

'How right I was, my darling girl, to want young Kavadis for you!'

Calanthe slipped her hand into Nik's, squeezing it as tightly as his was squeezing hers. She leant forward, brushed her father's cheek and smiled.

'Yes, Papa—so, very, very right,' she said.

'And I,' said Nikos, raising his glass again, 'completely agree.'

He lifted Calanthe's hand in his, brushing his lips across her knuckles. Then he clinked his glass against hers.

'To us both,' he said.

He glanced at Georgios, his father-in-law, then back at Calanthe. Love blazed in his face as he lowered their still-clasped hands to where, safe and secret within her, their baby was growing.

'To us *all*,' he said.

* * * * *